THOUGHT CATALOG BOOKS

Letters from Dinosaurs

Letters from Dinosaurs

LELAND CHEUK

Thought Catalog Books

Brooklyn, NY

Contents

Acknowledgements

I'd like to thank the editors who published the following stories in their journals:

"A Letter From Your Dinosaur" in *Tahoma Literary Review*

"Blacklights" in *Pif Magazine*

"First-Person Shooter" in *Lunch Ticket*

"Pyramid Schemes" in *Valparaiso Fiction Review*

"The Bullet Points of Valley Pete" in *Vol. 1 Brooklyn*

"League of Losers" in *Bartleby Snopes*

And thanks to *Salamander Magazine* for naming "Funeral By The Arcade" a finalist in the Salamander Fiction Prize, and thanks to *The Margins* for agreeing to publish it.

1

A Letter From Your Dinosaur

Dear Leland:

Thank you for the play you sent me for my birthday. I've never been much of a reader of plays, especially ones written by old white men. I find their brand of insistent, self-inflicted suffering difficult to relate to, but because I appreciate the gesture, I will not disparage your gift further.

You've proclaimed in recent interviews that you are a "self-made futurist." That my gratitude would appear to you in the form of a letter must seem quite obsolete, written on this flat-world mash of dried cellulose pulp, rather than typed and invisibly couriered via the now-hallowed institution of electronic mail (or worse, the computerized socialization mechanisms your generation worships). How "old-school" I am to rely on that horse and buggy, the Postal Service! What did you call me that time I visited you in college? A dinosaur?

I am doing well up here in Portland—thanks for asking. I know how much it pains you to call; I've read you much prefer texting. I don't leave the house much these days. Everything costs money and I have little. Remember when you told me,

"A career in education is a financial death sentence"? As if you needed to educate me, Mr. CEO of a Fancy Internet Company.

Now you're rolling your eyes. You tire of me bringing up financial issues. You believe in the American myth of social mobility. You like to think that you're a businessman whose creations make the world a better place. You tell journalists that your wealth is just a fortunate byproduct of your prodigious work ethic and God-given creativity. You tell journalists you'd be an entrepreneur for free; that's how passionate you are about your daily quest to improve the lives of others.

But when you were a child, you didn't want to go to Saturday Chinese school because you said, "Only poor kids who can't speak English go there." You only wanted to be friends with wealthy whites. By the time you were in middle school, you were selling baseball cards, keeping stacks of cash in one of my empty cigar boxes locked inside a desk drawer in your room. One day, you came home with a black eye because one of your customers discovered that his purchase was far from the mint condition you'd promised. You bragged that he hadn't seen the rounded corner because you'd sanded it down with an emery board. You claimed the boy's dissatisfaction was his own fault. Even in third grade, you believed in the theory, which many of your peers today espouse, that in business, cuckoldry is the fault of the cuckolded.

I wonder how an anecdote like that one would fit into your public relations agency's manicured narrative of the executive hero it spoon-feeds to the features editors of glossy business periodicals.

Speaking of narratives, last night I read what you sent me. *Look Back in Anger* by John Osborne. Did you choose that one because you think I'm angry and inert, like that ranting, working-class fellow Jimmy Porter? A rather obvious comparison, don't you think? Maybe you're right. I am angry. I haven't been able to find a job here, just as I failed in Spokane, Seattle, Eugene, and Boise. No teaching for dinosaurs.

Administrators take one look at me and practically sing that they'd rather hire someone young enough to be my grandchild. On my 70th birthday, I had a bowl of ramen for dinner, alone.

I'm thinking about driving to San Francisco for a visit. I feel that as I get older, I want to be close to my family. You probably think this is very selfish of me, since I abandoned your mother. I guess that's another commonality I share with that Jimmy Porter. We both loved someone outside our marriage. But I'll have you know that Karen, whom you've never asked after despite the fact that we were together for over twenty-five years, was the love of my life. That is, before she left me for that rich white poet last year.

I should never have married your mother. A friendship does not a marriage make. I never felt passionate love for her. Our union was something I thought I could endure. For you. Though my actions were not, my intentions were pure.

I apologize for insisting on not attending your wedding because of your wife's whiteness (and because, I think you would agree, she's also a bit overweight).

I'm sorry for neglecting to send a gift after the birth of your daughter, though in fairness, you've never sent me a photo of her, and I don't even know her name. I'm only aware of her because your mother mentioned the arrival of "her new granddaughter" in her annual eight-page, eight-packets-of-glitter holiday ramble.

I apologize for standing you up seven years ago when you were in Portland for business. The thought of you buying me dinner, laying down your corporate expense card before me like an Olympic medal, literally made me nauseous, so I unplugged my phone and stayed in for the night.

It is not without reservation that I plan to visit. I've never liked San Francisco and its love affair with its own mythologies. Even when it actually was the harbinger of a paradise that never materialized, it was only so for a segment of whites. As for today's San Francisco, the new and emerging utopia is a coin-operated one. Progressiveness is a luxury, energy-efficient car, a boutique, a green-built hotel, a solution for world hunger that pools the resources of the rich and exists only for those who drink the Internet like water.

You probably don't often hear this type of honest talk in your genteel, entrepreneurial circles. You're probably so offended that you're about to crumple this letter and throw it into your beloved talking platinum waste receptacle mentioned in that *Forbes* feature. You might even delicately slide these pages into your murmuring paper shredder, so evil these tree products have become. You look down on me like you looked down on the poor kids in Chinese school. You don't say that in your dull interviews about computer software and the World Wide Web, and you're probably afraid to say it to my face, but I know what you really think of me.

But you know what, Leland? I've grown softer with age. You'll see. I've been thinking a lot about grandchildren. In the same way that many women have very specific visions about their weddings, I've recently realized that I have always expected to have lots and lots of grandchildren. You know what's funny? Never imagined having children! Can't exactly have one without the other! No one ever said visions were required to make sense.

On the topic of making sense, it makes none that you hold your grudge against me in perpetuity. When I stay at your place, we must reconcile. I don't deserve your hatred, Leland. And you don't deserve to have me out of your life. The time for forgiveness is now.

I think about forgiveness every night before I go to sleep as I watch this rising pile of bills, as I dare not open the envelope I know to be an eviction notice. That's right, Leland. You always were a bright boy. You understand what this letter has been about all along. Mr. CEO of a Fancy Internet Company can make my bills vanish with a swipe of a card, and your coffers would hardly dent. You see, I'm not that dinosaur in that silly play. I understand what it means to be a citizen of your new and emerging utopia. We all must make money, and if we're not good at it, we must rely on those who are.

I envy your success. Does that make you feel better? I hope you remember that good feeling you just had. I hope you also ask yourself whether you've made your own, comparable mistakes, whether you've had your own personal indiscretions. And if the answer is yes or even maybe, then I hope you can begin to understand why I believe we can be father and son again.

Please reply and give up your anger, son.

Your dinosaur is coming to town.

2

Blacklights

"I don't like Doug's new girlfriend," Earl confessed.

His wife Grace lowered the oven's door and extracted a roasting pan of steaming sweet potatoes with mitted hands. "We don't even know her," she said, sighing loudly as she released the pan onto the stove with a clang.

Earl stared into the hot, black metallic maw and felt unsettled. He swirled a glass of red.

"Would you like some help?" he said.

"I'm done." Grace scooped potatoes onto a serving dish. "What don't you like about her?"

"Talks too much."

Several weeks ago, the four of them had taken a short walk in the park, and Earl's ears still rang from Laura's nattering. Oh, how taxing her dance performances were! Oh, what a grind, those commercial auditions! Earl and Doug had been best friends since kindergarten. They had gone to college and business school together. They ran a startup for three years before selling it to a public company. Of all of Doug's girlfriends (and there had been many), Laura was the most irritating. Earl tried to remember what she looked like. Blue eyes and blonde, but not from a bottle.

"Has to say every feeling that comes to her head," Earl said.

"You don't talk about your feelings at all," Grace said.

Her back was turned to him. She was washing the cutting board in the sink. The way her elbows churned, Grace looked like she was in the act of strangling someone. Was she still upset at Earl's cold reaction to her recently expressed desire to have children? Grace accused him of flip-flopping. Sure, he'd previously claimed to love kids. But was he being unreasonable to say that they were too expensive? She was a city social worker! Sure, they had a decent nest egg after selling the company. But none of Doug and Earl's latest ideas had taken off yet. What if none did? How would they manage then? No one liked to admit that having children could be an irreversible, life-altering mistake.

Grace emptied the sink and began to scrub it. She was growing her hair out again. He liked it long, so hearty, so dark—smelled of black figs. His sweet Grace. Earl wrapped an arm around her waist. They could overcome anything.

"Some feelings need not be said," he said, sliding his hand down to her backside.

Grace moved away. "For God's sake, Earl! Set the table."

Doug and his girlfriend arrived late, arms crooked and intertwined. The blushing Laura handed Earl a bottle of vodka. "Good to see you again," Earl said. She hugged him more tightly than he preferred. Earl inspected the clear glass, which was the color of faded clay against Laura's blonde hair. Vodka at a couple's dinner?

Doug was grinning sheepishly. "Sorry we're late." He glanced at Laura. "Traffic."

In the decades Earl and Doug had known each other before he started dating Laura, Doug had been tardy perhaps twice.

Unlike Earl's father, who was unreliable in every imaginable way due to his affinity for Pai Gow, Doug's father was big on discipline and structure; he was part of the Japanese civilian military before immigrating to the States. In the few times Earl had met Doug and Laura together, they'd been late each instance (not just a few minutes like today, but thirty, forty, fifty minutes). Earl imagined them stopping for sex in the car. Seemed like something they might do, something she might initiate. Earl vaguely recollected the time he and Grace had been so bold as to make love in an automobile. He practically had to get the community to sign waivers promising not to watch before Grace was comfortable.

"Your timing is perfect," Earl said. "Grace just finished cooking."

"No thanks to Earl," Grace said, smiling as she emerged from the kitchen. She hugged Doug and then Laura, kissing them on both cheeks. "Let's see if he can get you something to drink."

Grace was definitely still upset, Earl thought. He raised the bottle of vodka. "Well, there's no shortage."

Earl poured a very full glass of Bordeaux for Laura, who was already on glass number four. "Thanks, Earl," she said loudly, her blue eyes wide. He looked away so as not to be caught staring too long at her. Grace ladled sweet potatoes onto the plates of their guests.

"Every dish is so delicious," Laura said, her eyes rolling up on the words "every" and "so."

"It's been too long," Grace said. "Whenever Earl makes an effort to invite friends over, it's a special occasion."

"I make an effort." Earl forced a smile.

"As long as it doesn't cost you too much money," Grace said. "As long it doesn't take precious time away from your next ideation." Ideation: finger-quoted.

Doug laughed. Earl followed suit. "Apparently, it's not only the potatoes being roasted tonight," Earl said. "Someone should have told me ahead of time. I'd have worn a tweed jacket and bought a La-Z-Boy to sit in."

"Grace knows you can take it," Doug said, placing an arm around Laura. She squeezed Doug's thigh. Earl leaned over and kissed Grace's clammy cheek. The laboring oven had warmed the dining room to the point where the windows were fogged, frosting their view of the black night.

Laura slapped the table. "Oh my God! So here's why we're late."

Doug's eyes dropped. "It was no big deal."

"So we're at the liquor store," she said. "We're both standing at the counter. I pay for the vodka, and the owner looks at me, and then he looks at Doug and asks him, 'Can I help you?'"

"Why would he do that?" Earl said.

"He couldn't believe we were together!" Laura said. "When I told the guy Doug was my boyfriend, his face literally went white."

"Pun intended?" Earl said. Grace rolled her eyes.

"He actually said, 'Yes, ma'am,'" Laura said. "He called me 'ma'am!' He was so scared to admit his racism."

Doug rested fork on plate and swallowed with effort. "Maybe we weren't standing that close together."

"Sweetness!" Laura scooted her chair so that she and Doug touched thighs. "We were this close."

"Wow." Grace shook her head. "In this day and age."

Doug glanced at Earl, then Grace. He forced a smile and shrugged. "It happens."

"All the time," Laura said.

On the balcony overlooking the backyard, Doug set his near-full wine glass on the rail and lit Earl's cigarette. The outdoor light bulb had burnt out, and Earl kept forgetting to replace it, so the two men stood in near-darkness.

Doug had always been the man Earl wanted to be. Tall, thin, good-looking, well-spoken, perpetually genial. People were drawn to Doug. Earl considered himself short, a bit fleshy, generally undesirable to both women and men. When they ran the startup together, Earl led the engineering team, and Doug was the chief executive and spokesman to the media and the investors. He was good at saying the right thing and convincing people that he was genuine, a man of integrity. Someone in which you could invest with confidence. Earl was good at working long hours, coming up with ideas for his team to execute, observing workforce dynamics and maximizing non-optimal outcomes—avoiding the big mistake. Sure, Grace liked to ridicule Earl's cards-close-to-the-vest approach to life. But someone had to make sure what Doug sold was actually delivered upon. Only after selling the startup did Earl feel a modicum of relief, a tiny release, because he could pay off his undergraduate and graduate school loans. The college fund Earl's father had promised probably still sat in the coffers of some casino holding company.

At his wedding, Earl wept during Doug's best-man speech. He said that the two of them would be friends for life because

Earl saw things that Doug didn't; they were eyes on the same head, halves of the same heart. The touching nature of Doug's words—the emotion of the moment—surprised Earl.

"So what did you do to piss Grace off?" Doug said, grinning. "Too much time in the man den?"

"She thinks she wants kids," Earl said.

"That's great!"

"I don't."

"You don't?"

Earl shook his head. Doug laughed. "You guys have been married for ten years! How could there be a miscommunication about this?"

"Maybe I misled her," Earl said. "Misled may be strongly stated. I changed my mind. I like things the way they are." The truth? Saying you didn't want children seemed somewhat uncouth, especially when you knew your future wife wanted them. It was not unlike when he worked at a large corporation and his boss wanted Earl to drive a project that Earl knew was ill-fated. Do you tell your boss that her idea is ill-fated or do you put your personal feelings aside and do as told and act surprised when the aforementioned fate turns ill? Earl had never wanted to subject another human being to what he went through growing up. The bruising expectations of his mother. The frequent failings of his father. Their hypocrisy. The bullying. By boys and girls alike! Asian boys were never cool. And the Asian women! My, someone stop the white boy train! Perhaps progress had been made since Earl and Doug grew up. But was perhaps good enough?

"I think you two would enjoy parenthood," Doug said.

"Are you kidding?" Earl said. "I'm glad my parents are dead."

"Jesus, Earl."

"I know that sounds cold," Earl said, realizing that he wouldn't have said those words aloud if he were sober. "But that's the way I feel. That's the way lots of people feel. People want you to talk honestly about your feelings, but when you do, you're the asshole."

Doug said nothing for several seconds, brows hiked. "All I'm saying is, you've got a good woman there," he said. "Supportive. Patient. She put up with a lot during our boom days. You're a lucky dude."

"I am," Earl said, glancing inside at his tiny Grace chatting with statuesque Laura. "Absolutely, I am. Whatever it is that's bothering her, I'm sure it'll pass."

"What do you think of Laura?" Doug asked.

"She's fine, perfectly nice."

"I'm really head over heels," he said. "It's scary."

Earl looked up at Doug. Laura? Dramatic Laura? "That was quick," he said.

"Mistake?" Doug sipped his wine, his eyes still fixed on Earl.

He rested his elbows on the balcony's black steel rail and ashed his cigarette over the edge into the abyss that he knew to be his garden. The full moon was visible through the branches of the large, aged tree that walled off Earl's house from the neighbor's. His best friend was fishing for approval.

"I don't know her, really," he said, his voice tentative. "She's just so..."

"White?"

Earl laughed. "For the record, I was going to say 'animated.'"

"Like a cartoon."

"Stop."

"You don't like her," Doug said.

"That's not true." Earl wished he had brought his wine out with him as Doug had. His buzz needed re-sparking.

Doug again rested his wine glass on the rail. He touched Earl's shoulder and gently turned him away from the balcony's edge. Doug pointed at Earl's chest. "Tell me if I've lost my head. Not another joke. The truth."

Earl swallowed, uncomfortable with the scrutiny. He stared into the seemingly unending invisibility beyond them. He took a deep breath and sipped wine from Doug's glass. He cleared his throat and looked into his best and oldest friend's eyes.

"The liquor store incident," he said. "Does that happen a lot?"

Doug nodded. "I've dated white before, and I've never had these issues."

Doug told Earl that when he and Laura were alone together, it was great. Stellar sex life, relationship give and take, lots of common interests, and all that. But in public, Laura drew attention to herself—to the issue. He speculated that the attention came from her looks. She was an object of envy, perhaps. Earl pointed out that Doug had dated many good-looking women. ("Remember the Latvian-what-was-her name? Holy cow.") Earl theorized that the attention came from Laura's lack of subtlety, her enjoyment of confrontation. For that reason, Earl expressed his reservations about Doug's potential long-term commitment to Laura.

"She *prances*," Earl said.

When Earl and Doug returned to the women, Grace was sitting in a living room chair, and Laura was stooped over her, half-full wine glass in hand. Grace eyed the glass, frightened for her clothes and their furniture. Earl drifted toward Laura. She straightened and nearly hit Earl in the face with her glass and her many shiny bracelets.

"Let me freshen you up," Earl said, taking her weapon. He saw she was quite fit, possessed a dancer's effortlessly vertical posture. Earl teetered into the kitchen. He was pretty well buzzed.

Laura was practically singing about how her father, a Texan, had objected to Japanese Doug. That's what her father called him: Japanese Doug. Her father reasoned that if Laura stayed with Doug, his future grandchildren would never get to play high-school football because they'd be too short, even though Doug was five-foot-eleven.

"I won him over," Doug said. "I took him to a Cowboys game and knew all the players."

"He does like your earning potential," Laura said.

"He still thinks I'll find true love elsewhere."

"That is so awful," Grace said somberly.

"I think he'd have preferred that Laura brought home a Mexican," Doug said. "Then he could at least use his broken Spanish."

The conversation went out suddenly, as if someone had flipped a light switch. Earl pressed a throbbing spot in the orbit of his eye. It seemed everyone simultaneously realized that they were now discussing aloud topics better left unvoiced.

"Long story short, the man was calling me 'Son' by the end of our visit," Doug said. "I let him beat me at chess, too. He was so proud."

Instead of uncorking a new bottle of Bordeaux, Earl retrieved the vodka from the refrigerator and poured out several shot glasses. He knew Grace wouldn't approve; she wasn't much of a drinker. But Earl felt tonight was indeed becoming a vodka night, a night that would harken back to Earl and Doug's college days, when they attacked almost every situation with abandon, ignoring consequences. He peeked into the living room. Laura had finally stopped talking for the moment. She was sitting next to Doug on the couch, her shapely legs crossed and wagging, as if impatient, anticipating a dramatic moment. Choosing to ignore Grace's admonishing look, Earl rounded up the shot glasses and headed back to his guests.

Sitting in his living room armchair, Earl reached for Grace's hand. Perched on the arm of the couch, she left him hanging for a good thirty seconds before finally grabbing two fingers carelessly, without so much as looking at him. She might as well have flipped him a coaster.

Laura was now talking about how the bassist in her friend's band hit on her after every show even when Doug was in attendance. The bassist was black, Laura made a point of mentioning.

"I told Serge to back off last time," Doug said.

"He's so disrespectful," Laura said.

Earl wondered if her breasts (more than a handful) were natural.

"Makes you wonder if we're lucky, doesn't it?" Grace said to Earl.

"How's that?" Earl said, noticing the way Laura's short jacket and blouse exposed her creamy lower back as she reached down to tighten the straps of her heels.

"We're both Chinese," Grace said.

Earl looked over at Grace. Her breasts were smallish. Then he glanced at Laura, whose eyes were glassy from drink. Earl reminded himself to look at Doug, too.

"No one questions us," Earl said.

On the balcony, vodka and O.J. in hand, Earl struggled to hold the lighter steady enough to fire Doug's cigarette. Inside, Laura's voice rose over Grace's. Earl tried to glimpse Laura through the glass doors and couldn't see either woman. Doug took the lighter from Earl and lit his own smoke.

"I'm starting to see what you're saying," Doug said, smoke spouting from his lips.

Earl held up innocent, surrendering hands. "See? I'm not just being an asshole."

Doug stared skyward. He sighed. "I wish I had what you and Grace have," he said. "I'm tired of looking. Money changes things. And not for the better. It's harder to tell who really loves you."

Earl laughed. "Oh, come on."

Doug glanced at Earl, flat-lipped. "What?"

"Don't agonize over marriage," Earl said. "It's not a life sentence. You can always get divorced, so it's OK to look for something better."

Doug's head tilted, his lips parted slightly. "Does that mean you don't think of your marriage as a lifelong commitment?"

"Don't be absurd," Earl said. "I'm just saying that, unlike having children, marriage is reversible. Like if she can't shut her trap about how proud she is to date your non-whiteness, it's your right to walk away. Just like it's my right to walk if I don't like the way my marriage is going."

Doug began to say something, then stopped. He finished his cigarette and headed inside.

"What?" Earl said.

"Gotta piss, bro." Doug squeezed himself through the sliding glass doors before he had fully opened them.

Earl sipped his screwdriver and closed his eyes, relishing the warming of his frontal lobes. The wind picked up, raising the hairs on his arms. He looked down at the patches of reddened skin and realized he had been scratching all evening. Earl gazed down at his back garden, the egg-shaped shadows of the hedges wavering in the black. He was only speaking theoretically. He was taking himself out of the equation, a key to his success as a businessman and a key to his success in marriage. No one wins when you talk about your feelings. No one wins when you light the abyss, make visible the invisible. Perhaps he'd been a bit disrespectful to his marriage. Earl wasn't like Doug, though. He never fell head over heels for Grace. They just sort of happened. They happened to attend the same college, happened to be engineering majors, and their friendship just seemed to happen. Earl didn't like to admit that their courtship could have been considered arranged. Grace was the daughter of childhood friends of Earl's aunt and uncle, who lived in Shenzhen. Certainly, he didn't plan to discard his sweet Grace. Their life was happy. Grace always seemed to think more of Earl than he thought of himself, precisely because he avoided talking about his true feelings. But would he rule out divorce if she insisted on ruining their very comfortable existence by having a litter of money-eating dwarves (and they would be dwarves, thanks to Earl and Grace's below-average height)? No one liked to speak of it, but Earl was just being frank—blunt perhaps—ultimately honest. If Doug were to get serious with or perhaps even marry Laura, Doug would be making a mistake. He'd have his fun, but the things that bother you before marriage only magnify after. Like Grace's incessant criticisms, their sporadic sex life, her smallish breasts, and the fact she didn't wear makeup.

The glass door slid open. Laura staggered out. Her arms were bare; she had removed her jacket.

"It's cold out," Earl said.

"It is, isn't it?" Laura rubbed her toned, goose-pimpled arms. She reached in her pocket and pulled out a small spliff. "Mind if I smoke?"

Earl said nothing as he lit her joint. Seemed there wasn't an intoxicant Laura didn't like.

"Grace is a excellent cook," Laura said. "The potatoes just melted in my mouth." She stretched the words, saying them loudly as Earl heard Doug laughing with Grace inside. Laura's nipples were visible against her top.

"That's my Grace," Earl said.

"You have a chic house," Laura said. "Doug often says he'd love a place like this instead of the pad he has."

"We try to live a simple, modest life," Earl said, inhaling the secondhand pot smoke, trying to feed his inebriation. "We don't want to be targeted."

Laura laughed. "In this neighborhood?"

"Lots of Asian gangs," Earl joked. "You know how it is."

Laura shivered. "What do you mean?"

"Nothing." Earl drained his cocktail and turned toward the glass doors.

Laura grabbed his arm. "What did you mean?"

Her lashes were long, dark, and attention-grabbing thanks to her glittery mascara. Maybe she was blonde out of a bottle after all. Her lips were not so thin like other white women.

"You make race such a big issue," he said.

"What?"

"You've been talking about it all night," Earl said. "Constantly. You make it an issue with how you act."

"How do I act?" Laura said, her voice rising.

Earl clamped the back of his neck. No one wins when you talk. Laura repeated the question.

"Like you're the spokesman for our struggle or something," Earl blurted. "It's just silly."

Laura's face reddened and her features began to converge and strain and crease her heavily made-up skin. She was not nearly as attractive when angry. "I can't believe you would say that."

"Ask Doug," Earl said. "He agrees with me."

"You don't think I'm good for him," she said.

His eyes drifted toward a prominent mole near Laura's cleavage. Earl glanced inside, hoping to be rescued. Where were Grace and Doug? "That's not what I'm saying," he said, softening his voice. "I'm sorry I brought it up." He waited for the murmuring inside to commence. "Doug is a lucky man."

Laura licked her index finger and thumb and pinched out her joint. "You don't mean it."

"I do," Earl said quietly. "I'm sorry." He palmed her shoulder. Sinewy to the touch, not like soft Grace. He leaned in ever so slightly to whiff her blond hair. She smelled like sweat and crisp laundry.

Laura backed away. "I can tell you don't," she said. "Your wife says you lie all the time. About wanting kids. About not wanting kids. About what you like. About what you don't like. Doug and I don't have a perfect relationship, but maybe you should look at yours more closely."

Earl had stopped listening. Again, he moved in, nodding, his face close to hers, close enough to smell her boozy breath. Out of the corner of Earl's eye, he observed tall, thin Doug and little Grace talking, her face upturned. Footfalls on the hardwood. The slit of yellow glow between their dark figures. They were clearing the glasses from the living room. When was the last time Earl's pulse drummed this intensely? When was the last time he attacked a situation with abandon, cast aside caution? Back away, he told himself. His sweet Grace, his boy Doug.

He lowered his hand, wrapped an arm around Laura's waist, and pulled her close until their flanks touched. There was resistance, but Earl held firm. "I've always liked white women," he whispered into Laura's ear.

Earl and Grace stood in their front doorway, arms around each other. They bade their guests farewell. Grace promised to get on each other's calendars soon, and Earl reminded Doug to drive safely. Earl's hand was numb against Grace's flank. Would Laura mention their encounter on the deck? Christ, of course, she'd go on and on about it! Earl would have to explain himself. Would Doug forgive?

"What do you think of her now?" Grace asked, letting go of Earl, walking into the kitchen.

"As long as Doug loves her, I suppose," he muttered, following his wife. He rubbed his side where Laura had elbowed him. She had called him a number of ugly things. None could be construed as racist (save perhaps "limp dick"). He was lucky Grace had convinced him to splurge on double-paned glass for those sliding doors during last year's remodeling.

"What were you two talking about out there?'"

Earl peeked out the kitchen window, now streaked with dripping condensation, clearing a view of the black streets. "Nothing much," he said. Below, Doug opened the car door for Laura. He waved up at Earl. Earl held up a hand that felt like someone else's.

"Didn't seem like nothing." Grace turned on the faucet.

Her back was turned. She was rinsing a bowl in the sink. Her hair was tousled, ends frayed. She would soon say it was time for a cut. His Grace. No one would question them.

"She said they'd love to have what we have," Earl said.

"Did she?" Grace didn't turn around. Was she still upset at him? Earl wrapped his arms around her waist and placed his cheek against hers. He shut his eyes. Grace smelled milky, of sweat, her face cold. She wriggled free.

"What do we have, Earl?" she asked.

3

First-Person Shooter

Please, God, let today be like any other day. That's what I say every day before I get out of bed. That's what I've been saying every day for the past six years.

After I brush my teeth, I start my console, wear the headset, and log into a multiplayer. When Mom hears my clatter in the bathroom, she starts cooking. She's a really good cook. She's the only one in the family who gets me, understands why I've become what I've become.

In the multiplayer, I lie in the fuselage of a downed aircraft. My character, Sergeant James "Cobra" Caulfielder, groans. Outside, a soldier waves me forth, but before I can move, he's engulfed in a bulb of flame. My fellow soldiers shout "Move" repeatedly above a hail of weapon fire. The mission objectives crawl across the top of the screen. Enter the Fortress. Find and eliminate President. This is a particularly chaotic level of *End Times 2*, a very confusing map. I've tried it a few times and died.

Dying in a game is what I imagine dying in real life is like. The screen goes dark before you wake up again. Only in real dying, I hope you wake as someone else.

I go downstairs and eat with Mom in the kitchen. She's made chicken adobo. She pats me on the head, and I can tell she's not sure what to say next.

"What are you going to do today?" she says finally.

I shrug. She knows. Same thing I do every day.

"Maybe you should play some basketball in the backyard?"

"I don't like sports."

"I'm going to go to the mall with Aunt Theresa later—"

"No thanks."

"You can buy a new game."

"I can order them online."

Mom lets out a quick breath through her nose. She waddles slowly to the sink, plate in hand.

She's not happy with me. And that hurts. Nobody is happy with me. Mom and Dad and my older brother Steve say a lot of time has passed and people don't blame me anymore. Steve even tries to set me up with friends and girls and jobs.

They don't know what it's like. Nobody has ever blamed them. After that morning on campus with Eugene and after everyone found out that I was his only friend, I couldn't go outside without people and cameras staring at me, blaming me. That morning was so bright, the sky too clear. It was December. Where was the snow?

Some of the parents of the victims called me a murderer—just because I was Eugene's roommate. Once, on my way to class, one of the dead girl's dads stepped in front of me out of nowhere, and out of shock, I turned and ran. I got no more than a few steps before he grabbed my backpack and threw me to the ground. I stared up at him into the bright, cold sky. He shook me and the world reeled, looked fake. It was a new school year. Things were supposed to be better. The dad had tears in his eyes. Why? He kept asking. Why did Eugene kill his girl? He spat on me as he wept. He called me a few names about my race, but I don't want to make it about that. I don't blame him.

The parents of the kids who weren't shot that day were the worst. They tried to get me arrested as an accessory. They held signs outside our house and shouted at us. I remember my dad sitting at the dining table wearing his U.S. Navy hat, just staring off into space, as the chants went on for hours. He told me to go upstairs and stay there. I was watching television so I didn't want to move. My dad slammed a fist on the table and called me dumb and useless in Tagalog. I don't want to make it about what he called me. I don't blame him, either.

I live in a big house. When I'm not gaming, I work out in our home gym and watch the 70-inch high-def. I like older sitcoms best because they're usually filmed indoors. *Two and a Half Men, How I Met Your Mother, Friends.* I don't like reality shows, procedurals, or crime dramas—any show filmed outside. Sunlight makes people look too real.

I do lots of pull-ups, calisthenics, and butt exercises because I sit so much when I game. After lunch, I'm on the treadmill, watching Neil Patrick Harris talk about how awesome he is for the ten thousandth time. Mom walks in, holding the cordless.

"It's Steve," she says.

I stop the treadmill. "Aw, come on."

Mom continues to shake the phone at me. I take it.

"Hey, buddy," Steve says.

I hate it when he calls me buddy.

"Mom and I are thinking about taking you out to dinner tonight."

He says this like it's normal. Steve works at this company that does studies—the ones cited on the radio when there's not much news. Like that recent study that found that married working couples clean house less. Or the one that showed that people don't trust their neighbors.

I flip through channels until I find TV Land. *All in the Family* is on. It's the episode Archie gets put in lockup with commies and hippies. One of my favorites. I love how in sitcoms, the prisons always feel clean and comfortable, like even the set designers want to reassure us that they'll be out of jail in thirty minutes.

"Marcus?"

"Yeah?"

"Are you up for it?" Steve says.

I turn off the television and pull the shades down in the room. Mom is still standing there waiting to take the phone back. I shoo her away.

"What the fuck do you think?"

"Hey, language!" Steve says. "Do it for Mom. She deserves a break."

I want to give Mom a break. I don't want her to take care of me forever. She's getting old. I don't want to be a burden. I want to change. I just don't want to change *today*.

"I'm not like you, Steve. I'm not like you." My voice is rising. I'm shaking all over.

"OK, pal, OK," Steve says. "Calm down. Shhh."

I squeeze my eyes shut and force a few hard breaths. My teeth are clenched, and I can feel my pulse in my throat.

"Hey, did you know that studies show that toddlers bond with robots?" Steve says.

"Huh?"

"Nothing," Steve says. "Do you mind if Lily comes tonight?"

"Oh, Lord."

"Don't argue," Steve says. "Studies show that people who argue tend to get mad more often."

"Asshole."

"Language!" Steve barks. "You don't get everything you want in life, OK? Lily's part of the family, too. We're all sick and tired of walking on eggshells around you. Everyone knows what happened. So the hell what?"

Steve rarely gets angry. I feel like I might cry, so I swallow and pinch away the feeling.

"Look what you made me do," Steve says. He hangs up.

I go downstairs to give Mom the phone and see that her car is gone. She's left for Aunt Theresa's.

I return to the gym and continue my workout, lifting weights, doing pull-ups. The reason I don't like Steve's girl-friend Lily is that she's got the sensitivity of a brick. She always sends me job listings and offers to put me in touch with her "network," when we all know she's just an admin. She brings up my problem whenever she comes over. She often asks about what happened on that bright, crisp December morning six years ago like it was yesterday, like she's police. Yes, Eugene and I played a lot of video games. Yes, we'd been friends since we were seven. Yes, we liked first-person shoot-ers. Yes, I knew he had guns. Yes, I even filmed several of those famous videos where he's holding his guns and saying that he's going to kill the rich kids in school. I thought he was kidding around. Yes, when we walked to campus together that morn-ing, I noticed his backpack was fuller than normal. No, I never thought he would do what he did. No, I'm not a murderer, but you can call me one anyway. I won't get mad. I'm used to it.

I see myself walking to class with Eugene. I told him about the first *Halo*, about how I thought the game was a cautionary tale about the separation of church and state. He nodded and smiled, but he wasn't really listening. We were crossing the quad. Students were going to class. The campus shuttles dropped off a large group. We passed a big oak tree, and Eugene pushed me behind it and said to get down, stay down, and stay there. He was protecting me, like someone was attacking us. He slung his backpack over his chest and ran toward one of the buildings. Entered the fortress. Soon, the screams, the gunshots.

I fall off the pull-up bar and land on my hands and knees. My arms are fried. I've been doing pull-ups for ten minutes. I shower, go to my room, lock the door, and start up my console. I enter another multiplayer on *End Times 2*. It's a map of the planet Gurkanus. The objective is to rescue a prisoner from a home nestled in a crowded interplanetary version of a favela called an Argento. Lots of blind alleys and mosquito-like aliens. Of course, we're in the middle of a war as well, and the Argento is getting bombed. We have to listen for the air growl, the scene to shudder, the sign to take cover. Chaos.

Sometimes I imagine one of the other players on my side is Eugene. People didn't believe me when I said that Eugene was a good guy. Back when we were in high school, he helped his parents out at the dry cleaners every day after school. When we played fighting games, he'd let me win. We were ten when we filmed a short movie on a camcorder. He played a black-hooded-and-caped superhero named Obsidian Man, and I played a white-masked bad guy named Chalk. While we filmed a fight scene, he accidentally split my lip with a punch and was so upset about it that he started crying.

I was the one who introduced him to gaming in the first place. I got him into military shooters. *Call of Duty. Battlefield. Metal Gear Solid.* I can't play those games anymore. Can't do real guns.

Neither of us liked college. I think he had a crush on this white girl Brittany who was way out of his league. She's an actress now on one of those shitty USA Network shows.

People used to tease us. They called us Gay Nerds. Eugene had a bad stutter that made him put F sounds on everything. I used to be thin and gangly, and I wore really thick glasses. Eugene and I weren't good at much of anything really, other than sitting in front of a screen and pressing buttons on a piece of plastic.

"Did you know you can order one of those online?" Eugene said one night while we were playing *Call of Duty.*

"One of what?"

"The assault rifle, the M4A1," he said. "Full-auto fire. You can even get one with a sight."

In *End Times 2,* I've found the prisoner hiding beneath a sewer grate. He's a dark-haired fellow. Emaciated and gangly like I used to be. He holds some secret about President. At the other end of this Argento is our escapecraft. I've got to blast aliens to protect him. I ask the other players to cover me. We get to the ship. Off into the atmosphere we go. The planet grows visible through the window. Fade out. The players exchange congratulations over headsets. We're all strangers, but I imagine that this is what the congratulations would have felt like had I been a hero that December morning instead of just another dumb coward hiding behind a tree. Once I realized what was happening, I should have gone after Eugene. I'd like to believe that he wouldn't have been able to look me, his best friend, in the eye and kill me.

I log off and drift through the silent and empty house. Mom's been gone for an hour, and I already miss her. In the backyard, the sky makes our lawn look plastic. There's a deck, a patio, and a grill that's layered with dust. I slide open the glass door and touch the fly screen. How easy would it be to pull the screen aside and step out into the real world again? I look beyond our fences, and even though I know no one is watching me, I feel eyes peering through the cracks, judging me, and my guts clench. I hurry to the kitchen and brace myself against the sink, the nausea. Once the feelings pass, I down a glass of water.

The garage door groans open. Mom's back. I shut the sliding glass and close the vertical blinds. I feel whole again. She's moving slowly, carrying four full paper shopping bags. I take them all from her. I start emptying the groceries, putting proteins in the fridge, canned foods in the pantry. Mom isn't saying anything, and she isn't looking at me. Is she still upset?

I ask her if she's OK.

Her glance doesn't linger. She's ashamed of me. She lowers herself into a chair and mops her brow. "Just tired," she says. Then she asks if I'm hungry. I tell her I am.

I wait in the living room while Mom shuffles to the stove to make me a snack. I find an old episode of *Facts of Life* on TV. I'm not a good person. I'm a burden. I should be doing more with my life. Eugene and I were computer science majors. We never finished.

Soon, the smells rise from my mother's wok. Fried soy sauce noodles with bok choy—that's my guess. My stomach growls. The inside of my mouth moistens. I've never offered to help Mom cook.

"Dad called," she says. Mom rarely mentions Dad. He spends most of the time over at the apartment building he manages. He's given up on me. I can't remember the last time he asked how I was doing. "He wants to go out to dinner tonight."

"What am I going to do?"

Mom didn't look at me. "He wants you to come." She plates my snack and sticks it in front of me like bad papers she wants me to sign. "Marcus, it's time."

I tell her no again, grab my plate, and storm upstairs.

"Dad will be at the restaurant!" Mom shouts. "He'll be waiting! We will be waiting!"

Her shrillness makes me nauseous. I can't remember the last time she raised her voice. I lock myself in my room and eat in front of my television. The noodles are tasteless. Mom's cooking is usually so good. This dish is slopped together. Barely any soy sauce at all, and the bok choy are wrinkled. The steps creak. She's making her way upstairs. I start up the console.

I hear Mom talking on the phone. She's speaking Tagalog in a high-strung, plaintive tone, which means she's talking to Dad. "I told you we should have sent him to someone," says Mom. My dad didn't think I should get professional help because I was healthy and young.

The screen comes up, but everything goes out of focus. I put my forehead to the ground and cover my ears. My eyes are squeezed shut, and I'm rocking back and forth and screaming silently. I'm beyond hope. Twenty-six years old, and my life is over. I think Eugene spared me because I was supposed to live the life he wished he had the courage to lead. But what have I done with his favor? I know how people my age are supposed to be. I'm supposed to be like Steve. I'm supposed to have goals and responsibilities. I'm not supposed to have Mom practically wipe my butt for me. I'm supposed to make Dad proud of my accomplishments. But even if the shooting hadn't happened, I feel like I'd be like this. I know I'm not normal. We'd have a normal family except for me. Eugene should have killed me, too. Then I could wake up and be someone else.

I haven't heard a sound in the house for some time. I go downstairs, back upstairs, then downstairs. Mom's gone again. I see her note on the whiteboard.

"Walking to Olive Garden. Meet you there at 5:30."

We live in the suburbs. Olive Garden is probably two hours away by foot, underneath freeway overpasses and over train tracks. Mom is 61 and overweight, and she takes medication for hypertension and high cholesterol.

The phone rings. I pick up.

"What did you do?" Steve says.

"What?"

"Mom says she's walking to Olive Garden."

"I know!"

"Is she insane?"

"You've got to get her."

"I've got to work," Steve says. "I know you're unfamiliar

with the concept, but I can't just up and walk out. You have to get her."

"Where's Dad?"

"How am I supposed to know? Maybe he's walking to Olive Garden, too."

"I haven't driven in six years."

"It's like a bicycle," Steve says.

"Fuck you."

"Studies show that you can put a key in an automobile, put the joystick in reverse, and find your mother," Steve says. "Call me back when you've found her."

He hangs up, and I shout expletives. I grab the car keys and open the door that leads to the garage. I dry-heave, feel dizzy as the daylight washes over the car, stinging my eyes. More expletives. Some whimpering. Lots of sweating. I step out of the house like I'm going over a cliff. My feet hit the concrete and squish a little, and I put my hands out and brace myself against the hood of Mom's minivan. Why is she doing this to me?

I'm making noises I've never heard from myself as I approach the driver's seat. I hear the screaming of the students that day. They sound like locusts in my memory now. My whole body shakes as I pop the door open and slide into the seat. I feel like I'm squeezing myself into a baby's chair. I can hardly move. My thighs are indented by the steering wheel. I try to find the button to slide back, but I end up shifting the mirrors, the windshield wipers, the digital clock—everything but the seat. Then I find the bar below the chair. It's manual, old, like my parents. I put the key in the ignition. I'm a mess. I'm drooling a little, snarling, crying. I turn the key. The minivan roars. I put the gearshift in reverse, shut my eyes, and lower the right foot. Scream. Scream so I can't hear the neighbors calling me names.

The van shoots into the street, screeching as I slam the brakes. I almost hit a neighbor's mailbox. I take a breath and am surprised I still feel OK. Tell myself this is just like a video game. Then I proceed slowly. When I start a new video game, I usually go all out right away, charging into traps. If I die in a game, I just start over. Learn. Get better. Why can't I do that in real life?

I'm moving about fifteen miles per hour on our empty road. I eye the sidewalks. No Mom. I try to remember the way to Olive Garden. It's a right, then a left on the expressway, and you go like ten miles. Mom can't be far. I jerk the car to the left, and it overturns, so I jerk back to the right, and I'm swerving as I get to the stoplight, which turns green so I have to go. My foot drops on the pedal too hard, and I'm off into the intersection, plowing onto a four-lane boulevard. I'm sweating through my shirt. I scan for Mom's round figure, her specific waddle. She should stand out against the concrete nothingness that Eugene railed against in his video.

"I just want to feel something good in this wasteland," he hissed, pointing those guns at the camera. "The world is ugly like me."

I stop at a light. I feel unbalanced, like I'm sitting in a boat. I've never actually been in a real boat. I rowed a boat onto the shores of Normandy in a WWII shooter. I see myself running across the quad again after the gunshots stopped. Four or five students gaped at the ground, crying and screaming ohmyGods. I'm tall so I could see over them. A girl lay there.

A brunette, but we can't recognize her. She'd been shot in the face.

I hear a horn. I've been sitting in front of the green light for too long. My move. The horns sound again. I dry-heave. Cars swerve around me. I hit the hazard lights. They said I was a hazard to the community.

Then I see Mom. Looking so alone on the sidewalk. The overpass and freeway on-ramp in the distance. I pull up beside her and roll down the passenger side window. Though she's red-eyed from crying, she looks at me like I'm someone new.

It's 5:30. We park in front of Olive Garden, and I step out of the car. The first couple of steps are a little mushy, like the asphalt has turned to rain-softened soil. The next steps are steadier, and I begin to think I'm getting better. I can breathe. No one is looking at me and thinking about what happened that December day years ago. Mom takes the crook of my elbow, and we're walking together, outside, like this happens all the time, like we're normal. As long as she's with me, I'll be OK.

Inside the restaurant, Dad is seated at the head of the table. He is wearing his U.S. Navy hat with the flat brim as usual. He adjusts his tinted glasses. He's probably thinking I'm a mirage. He's surprised I've made it, like he was surprised I made it after he heard news of the shooting on the radio. He always expects the worst so he can avoid disappointment. Mom kisses him on the cheek, and she whispers something to him. Dad continues to stare at me, his lips parted by amazement. I sit across from Mom. I'm still in wet gym clothes. A mess. I've been through chaos, but I'm here.

"I'm proud of you," Dad says. "You've always been so smart. I remember teaching you long division when you were three. You got it right away."

His chin trembles, and he's fighting back tears, so I'm fighting back tears. Dad has spoken more to me in the last five minutes than he has in five months. Mom takes Dad's cell phone and calls Steve to tell him and Lily to come. She has to repeat herself three times.

Today is the seventh anniversary of the shooting. Eugene shot 34 students, then himself. People used to tease us. They called us Gay Nerds. Eugene had a bad stutter that made him put F sounds on everything. I used to be thin and gangly, and I wore really thick glasses. Eugene and I weren't good at much really, other than first-person shooters. This is what I tell Jessica, my therapist, as we walk around Dailybrook, the place I go twice a week.

"Mom and Dad are on a cruise," I tell her.

Jessica puts her hand on my shoulder. A line appears between her brows and vanishes. "Do you feel deserted?"

We are standing in the quad of Dailybrook, under a large tree, like the one at the college. I think of Eugene.

"Not by them," I say.

4

1776

Late at night, in the lobby of the headquarters of Globe, Incorporated, Jerry feather-dusts the framed black-and-white stills of the company's buildings in Hong Kong, Tokyo, Paris, and Sydney. In the photos, the sky is clear though the streets are wet; the clouds have been digitally removed. Faint halos crown the buildings. On the streets, there are a few tiny human figures, obfuscated to provide the appearance of motion and speed. The blurs look like squashed ants. Jerry tilts his head right and left; altered perspective might help him view the figures with clarity. That's when he sees the sticker on the bottom of the frame. Tiny, fits on the side of a finger.

"1776," white letters against black.

How did that get there, and what does it mean?

Jerry is new to Globe, a half-century-old telecom company that was founded in America, funded by a Russian private equity firm started by the sons of oil oligarchs, merged with an Indian conglomerate, and most recently, acquired by a Chinese company. The board (which consists of three Russians, six Chinese, five Indians, and one American) installed a new management team three years ago that championed a reorganization initiative to promote global collaboration. The company moved its headquarters to Globe City, a man-made island just south of Singapore, and a select group of employees were relocated there. In this tower, floors one to twenty-two are populated by Russians, twenty-three to forty-four by the Chinese, forty-five to sixty-six by the Indians. Employees are encouraged to speak their native tongues. When visiting a foreign floor, employees should have the requisite amount of cultural respect to speak a few words of the language-of-record on that level. Jerry works where the employees speak English, where the Americans work: the basement.

The stickers appear on more places. On a john on an India floor, on the back of a flat screen on a China level. Employees ask one another whether they plan to walk out on January 7th. 1776 references the date: January 7, 2076. Jerry passes a foursome of Americans; they are huddled and whispering. As Jerry walks by, they go silent. Their eyes follow him. They wait for him to turn the corner before they resume speaking. But they are too late. Jerry has already heard them say that a walkout is not enough.

Jerry is an experiment. His bowl-shaped black haircut is a perfect half-sphere leveled at the ear tops—the mark of a rehabilitant. He doesn't remember where he's from or from what he has been rehabilitated. May have been any and many a thing: abusing drugs, viewing pornography, gambling in excess, threatening a politician, corporate executive, or law enforcement officer, spewing racial epithets, driving under the influence, or engaging in a long list of other behaviors judged antisocial. An unwavering daily routine of vitamins, group and individual therapy, strenuous exercise, light depri-

vation, and in tougher cases, heavy doses of myriad pharma-
ceuticals gradually erases a rehabilitant's memory. After the
first year, a rehabilitant undergoes further testing to ensure
he never remembers why he entered The House. Those who
remember too much must remain. Those who remember too
much when Outside must return. The House places the rehabilitant at a company to fill openings for those who do not
mind performing menial tasks for a low wage. According to
the press releases, the rehabilitant placement program has
been an unmitigated success. The House's customer base is
highly satisfied as evidenced by the survey data, testimonials
from well-known executives, and the steady growth of both
the number of customers and the reputability of said customers. After going public in America five years ago, the company has opened satellite operations in thirty-five countries in
Asia, North America, and Europe.

Jerry's manager is named Charry. He is short with curly
brown hair. He wears a yarmulke and a badge with four names
on it (Cziktor, Cha Ren, Chandrasekhan, Charry), one for
each floor group. Charry has worked at Globe since the India
merger two decades ago. He has seen various new management teams tout initiatives that promised big accomplishments that ranged from quadrupling profitability to changing
the world for the better. He knows that the initiatives and their
objectives are not as important as standing behind whoever
is in charge and maximizing one's odds of surviving the next
purge when it inevitably comes. When the Chinese took over,
Charry didn't complain, and when the janitors were down-
sized, he was promoted to SLoJWaF (Senior Leader of Jani-

tors, Windows, and Food). He received an office (converted broom closet) and began managing a small team.

Back then, each floor was cleaned by five janitors several times per day. Now there are only a handful of custodians left, and they are each responsible for cleaning five to ten floors. They share several lockers in the row where the window washers and food service contractors dress. When Charry's boss retired, Charry obtained approvals to enlist The House for contract resources.

Charry likes Jerry. Jerry is obedient. He works hard. He doesn't concern himself with which country works on which floor and whether that's good or bad. Charry coaches Jerry on how to be a good janitor, how to hold the broom lightly to avoid calluses, and which cleaning agents work best on the darkest of stains. Charry invites Jerry to his office at least once a week, and they eat their cafeteria-delivered bag lunches together. One day, while eating, Charry asks how Jerry has liked his first month at Globe.

"I enjoy the newness," he says. "The learning."

"The House speaks very highly of you."

"Do you know Mentor?"

Charry nods, even though he doesn't. The House's Rehabilitant Managerial eToolbox recommends that managers identify closely with the rehabilitant's mentor to smooth assimilation. "Mentor is a good man," he adds.

"I wouldn't have been ready for placement without him."

"Everyone deserves a fresh start," Charry says. The House recommends dangling tangible and intangible rewards to motivate the rehabilitant. "If I were to tell you that you are outperforming many of your fellow Americans, what would you say?"

"I would say that I expect to succeed," Jerry replies.

Charry chuckles inadvertently. Jerry has responded exactly as the eToolbox predicted.

"Did I say something funny?" Jerry says.

Charry shakes his head. "You are doing a great job."

"Am I outperforming my peers?"

"Didn't I just tell you so?"

"No," he says. "You said 'if.' Conditional."

Charry is surprised by the exasperation in Jerry's voice, the sharpness. The House promises to place "employees unafraid of competing in today's global economy."

"Mentor did a good job on you," Charry says.

On a bright, clear Sunday, Jerry takes a bus to The House for his monthly check-in with Mentor. He enters through the familiar ivy-covered gates. Inside, he feels safe. The smell of aged wood relaxes him. The high, vaulted ceilings and the light bursting through stained glass fills him with a feeling that a higher, benevolent force guides us all. The bespectacled receptionist smiles and asks if he has a scheduled meeting. Jerry nods and shuffles quickly into the booth in the far corner of the lobby. He jerks the door shut, clicks on the purple light, and eyes the intercom box perched on a plinth. He sits in the chair, takes a deep breath, and straightens his bangs before flipping the box's switch.

"Welcome back, Jerry," Mentor says. "How is it Outside?"

"I like it very much."

"I sense that you are not telling the whole truth."

Jerry wishes he hadn't lied. In The House, he wouldn't have. But Outside, people expect you to say certain things, even if untrue, to make them feel better. "Life is simpler here."

"Complexity is a reward," Mentor says.

Jerry retrieves a notebook from his backpack and writes down Mentor's words.

"What is bothering you, Jerry?"

"I sense that some workers don't like Globe," Jerry says. "Some want more."

"It is convenient to assume that our leaders are detached and stratified, and that their aim in our glorious global economy is simply to accrue wealth, and that they don't care about you, the worker," Mentor says. "When we were children, they called us Americans 'leaders of the free world.'" He laughs quietly to himself. "My parents presumed foreigners lacked their aptitude and their values, but most importantly, their will to compete. But they were wrong. Now Americans are only special because they make the best janitors and window washers; they know how to keep things clean. When you leave here, people will underestimate you because you are a rehabilitant and because you're from America. They will think that you lack their aptitude and that you are easily manipulated and that your past has ruined your future. But one day, you may own what used to be theirs. You're not the typical American anymore. You have the hunger to learn. You don't expect the world to feed you. You have the will to compete at the global level, Jerry. He who does not want to compete must accept his place in line."

Jerry again writes the words down. "He who does not want to compete must accept his place in line," he reads aloud.

Jerry lives in a studio in Singapore in what used to be a government housing complex that The House has purchased for its placements. A shuttle takes Jerry and his fellow rehabilitants to and from the ferry each day. Jerry is out of his studio by 7 AM and back by midnight. By design, the apartments, ferries, and shuttles do not have reflective surfaces. No glass fixtures, no mirrors, no stainless steel, no glossy finishes. Jerry would not have noticed this unusual limitation had he not seen the framed stills in the Globe office lobby. When he saw the dark reflected arc of his head in the glass, he observed himself in third-person, and it felt like a memory.

Since that day, Jerry has been looking to sneak home objects that might provide a reflective surface to see his face. Tonight, he has brought the rod of a brushed nickel toilet roll holder. Its finish doesn't appear glossy but Jerry hypothesizes that he can burnish it with a dab of one of his cleaning agents and a harsh sponge to get the metal to reflect. He uses up an entire travel-sized bottle of cleaning fluid but still cannot see his face in the surface.

The basement receives a memo. Effective January 1st, all floor badges belonging to Americans who are not janitors, window washers, or food service workers will cease to have access to the numbered floors. No reason is given. The Americans are concerned. Does this mean they will be let go? If they are let go, will they receive severance? How will the severance amount compare to what they would have received in America? Did someone tip off management about the planned walkout, about 1776? Is this retaliation?

A few of the Americans separate themselves from the crowd in the workroom. Jerry observes them huddling, chattering passively like spectators of a soccer match, the results of which they cared very much about but could not be bothered to affect.

The next day, the group fails to appear at work. Jerry hears that they've been let go.

The basement is especially unproductive for the rest of the week. The Americans who are not janitors, window washers, or food service workers number in the hundreds. They are a motley mob of accounting clerks, internal help desk representatives, and garbage and recycling sorters. A few continue to speak loudly against the harshness of management's methods. One morning as they put on their uniforms, Charry tells Jerry to keep his head down and not to worry.

"It'll pass," Charry says.

Jerry nods. "If they are let go, it will be because they didn't want to compete."

Charry's forehead pleats, but he says nothing.

On Christmas Eve, Jerry cleans a China floor. By far, the worst restroom he's serviced. He puts on his mask and sprays the hole in the ground. A bleach steam rises. From outside the stall, he probes beneath the footpads with his mop. The Russians have their weak flush, and the Indians prefer their overhead chains, but at least they use Western toilets.

One of the Chinese employees steps past Jerry's orange "wet floor" cone ("Wet Floor" is also translated into four languages). The man stomps all over the freshly mopped tiles, leaving a zigzagging fleet of dress shoe prints. He enters the stall Jerry has just cleaned and begins to hose it down with fresh, crackling urine. When he's done, he closes a nostril with a finger and unloads a thick rope of mucus. Then he kicks over the cone on the way out.

Jerry reminds himself to keep working, without excuses, without complaint. The Chinese man does not intend disrespect. It is Jerry's job to clean that stall again. He bends over and uprights the cone. A widespread pair of polished black boots becomes visible on the threshold. The American's strawberry blonde hair is slicked back and shiny with pomade. He is one of the men Jerry saw huddling the day before. The names on his floor badge are stacked one on top of the next: Pyotr, Pei Der, Parekh, Peter.

"Jerry?" he says, reading his badge. He peeks over his shoulder, checking for surveillance. "Do you know about 1776?"

Jerry looks down at himself, then at Peter, then at the mop prostrate on the ground and his cleaning supplies scattered around the janitorial truck.

"We don't deserve to be in the basement," Peter says. "We don't deserve to be treated like we don't exist. We deserve opportunities." He waits for a response but Jerry is expressionless.

"Do you understand the significance of 1776?" Peter says.

Jerry shakes his head.

"Not much American History Inside, huh?"

Jerry tries to remember. "I don't know."

Peter shakes his head. "I hear they teach you thirty different languages and eight different religions."

"I only know English."

Peter purses his lips and scrutinizes Jerry. "I think it's terrible what The House does to you. Americans are a uniquely tolerant people, not like the Chinese and the Russians. Wait, you are an American, right? I just assumed, since you work in the basement."

Jerry nods.

"Oh, good." Peter glances over his shoulder again. "The Chinese are the worst. Boorish. Like animals."

Peter imitates a Chinese person speaking heavily accented English and laughs at his own impression. Jerry tunes out, gathers his cleaning supplies, and arranges them on his cart.

"Hey, I'm not offending you, am I?" Peter says. "Are you Chinese? Or are your parents Chinese? I can't tell. You look kind of Eastern. But you speak American English."

"I don't remember where I'm from."

"And we don't care," Peter says. "Because we're Americans! Listen, we have to do something to get Globe's attention. This badge thing doesn't bode well. They just canned a bunch of my friends. You could be next." Peter tells Jerry that the 1776'ers are plotting more than an organized walkout. Almost every American in the basement has a role. The window washers are going to open the windows of each level one by one, from the China floors on up. The Americans will enter the numbered floors from the freight elevators and empty the contents of each floor (computers, chairs, desks, etc.) out the windows.

"Like the Boston Tea Party," Peter says.

"A tea party?"

"Never mind," he says. "We need your help. Once our badges are deactivated, you guys in the locker room will have the only cards with access to the numbered floors. Charry doesn't like me. And neither does the rest of those guys."

"I don't want to get in trouble," Jerry says.

"No one will know," Peter says. "Just leave it in your locker when you and Charry are having lunch. Done. Easy."

Jerry keeps his head down. He finds Peter vaguely distasteful but can't articulate why.

"Do you like it here?" asks Peter.

Jerry blinks rapidly, uncontrollably. "No one on the numbered floors talks to me."

Peter inhales and nods. He squeezes Jerry's shoulder. "I don't like it here, either."

His watch beeps and he turns to leave. "You don't have to answer me now," Peter says.

Charry opens the fridge and removes two bag lunches: his and Jerry's. He walks into his office and sits behind his desk, waiting for Jerry to complete his morning rounds. Jerry is very close to the perfect employee: a machine that routinely puts in fifteen-hour days, sometimes squeezing in seven or eight cleanings of his assigned floors. Charry is beginning to feel like he can do less and Jerry can take on more. Also, because Jerry has done so well, Charry looks better to management since he was the one who first suggested Globe use The House's placement program. If there were ten Jerrys, you could fire the remaining tenured janitors and save on the salaries and benefits. If Charry continues to demonstrate this capacity for forward thinking, management might even put him in charge of the entire floor.

Jerry appears in the doorway. His brow is furrowed and his shoulders are hunched. "Someone took my lunch," he says.

Charry smiles and raises Jerry's brown bag before laying it on the desk.

Jerry sits and tears open the bag; the plastic-wrapped sandwich and apple spill onto the desktop. He unwraps the sandwich and takes a big bite. Charry watches as Jerry barely stops to breathe while eating.

"Did you have breakfast today?"

Jerry nods, biting into his apple. "I did double the rounds."

Charry's eyes widened. Ten floors in three hours. "Did you rush?"

Jerry shook his head and hands over a stack of punch cards. Charry flips through them. All are completed.

"Am I outperforming my peers?" asks Jerry.

Charry laughs. "You are."

Jerry allows himself a smile. Charry considers a reward. But there are very few incentives to give an employee of Jerry's level and tenure. Much too early for promotions. Far too low-level for spot bonuses. Charry waited nearly seven years for his first promotion. But he has an idea.

"Jerry," Charry says. "I want to show you something." He points to the file cabinet beside his desk. "Look in there."

Jerry opens the cabinet. In hanging folders with numbered tabs, the floor plans.

"How many floors are there?" Charry asks.

"Sixty-six," Jerry says without looking.

Charry crosses his legs, and his black rubber shoes sway back and forth. "Look again."

Jerry gets to the last of the folders, and there are a series of blank pages numbered sixty-seven. "There's a sixty-seventh floor?"

Charry places a finger to closed, smiling lips.

"What's up there?" Jerry asks.

"Since you've been doing such a good job, why don't you go up there and find out?"

"Really?" Jerry beams.

"Yes, really," Charry says. "Only a select few have been allowed to clean the sixty-seventh floor. My manager gave me the privilege after many years here. You've earned the reward in just over a month."

Jerry looks in Charry's eyes and says, "One day, you may own what used to be theirs."

Charry flushes. Jerry seems to expect him to recognize some sort of reference. "Yes, Jerry, I might," he says. "Well, not likely. But I'd love to have greater responsibility here at Globe."

"No," Jerry says. "I mean, me. I might own what used to be theirs if I work hard and don't expect the world to feed me. That's what Mentor said."

"Ah," Charry says, still not sure exactly what Jerry is talking about. "Yes, that's what people say."

The next day, before he starts working his way down to the numbered floors, Jerry takes the freight elevator up from sixty-six. The floor is unmarked. The entrance is crisscrossed with yellow caution stripes. He places an ear against the door and hears nothing. There is a black globe above him, a camera. He slides his badge over the reader and enters.

He pushes his sloshing cart down a hall with offices on either side, lit by dull gray sky through windows. The walls are soundproof glass. Behind the walls, there are dozens of people in suits, talking on earpieces. One of the offices appears to be a weightless chamber. Inside, a woman floats about, seemingly mouthing to no one. Beyond the conference rooms, there's a firing range. Jerry feels dull reverberations in the pit of his stomach as ear-plugged men shoot at targets.

Jerry stops at the end of the hall, in front of slate double doors marked Barracks, and looks back again at what surrounds him: the authority, the might. No matter how many people Globe employs, the central nervous system of the corporation is right here on the sixty-seventh floor. Mentor had said that one day, because of his will to compete, Jerry would move to the front of the line. The people here own what the Americans in the basement once owned.

Jerry enters the barracks. Bunk beds stretch as far as he can see. Gun racks line the walls. Two men in dark navy-colored uniforms wrestle on a bed. Another duo twirls pistols and points them at each other. Seated at a folding table in an aisle, a foursome plays cards and takes shots of liquor. All men. Indians, Americans, Chinese, Russians, Arabs. Maybe fifty in all. No one sees Jerry, even as he openly observes them.

A gunshot makes Jerry flinch. Behind him, a groan. "Call me a bitch again, bitch!" someone yells. The card players abandon their game and stagger past Jerry toward the fracas, hooting and hollering. More shots are fired. Men laugh.

Jerry pushes his cart toward the bathrooms.

The bathrooms. Those on the sixty-seventh floor piss and shit and puke and ejaculate and bleed (sometimes all in one stall) like animals. Many, many times worse than the China floors. The mask Jerry places over his mouth, he wishes he could place over his eyes.

One stall is dimmer than Jerry expects. He's reminded of

Mentor's booth. The overhead light fixture has been smeared with feces.

Two stalls over, Jerry discovers one guard fellating another at gunpoint.

In the next, a guard weeps quietly while talking on the phone. He pleads for a chance to go home.

Jerry suppresses his fear and revulsion and follows the checklist, marks the punch cards, and waits for the stalls to empty before dutifully cleaning each of them.

He finds a lid that has broken free of its toilet paper holder. It's a polished chrome panel the size of a slice of American cheese. Jerry can see a distorted version of part of his face. He slides the lid into his pocket.

Jerry keeps his head down and hurries to the exit. Before he reaches the door, Jerry is grabbed by the arm. The guard has a strong grip, a shaved head, and dark blue eyes.

"What happened to Charry?" he says.

"He sent me today."

The guard releases Jerry's arm. "Charry's a good man."

Jerry nods. "He's helped me a lot."

He can feel himself beginning to blink uncontrollably. He turns his right hip—heavy with the toilet paper lid—away from the guard.

"What do you think of 1776?" asks the guard. He looks Jerry up and down, his hand brushing his holster.

"Charry told me to keep my head down."

Smiling, the guard pats Jerry on the head. "Thanks for cleaning up after us."

"It's my job."

"The boys in here are savages," the guard says. "Not me,

though. I try to be clean and respectful. Everyone's job is inter-connected, you know? Your job allows me to do my job, and my job allows someone else to do his."

Jerry nods. "I know that if I work hard and don't make excuses, I can own this one day."

The guard laughs. "Charry has really done a good job on you."

"It is a privilege to clean this floor," Jerry says. "You are the first person on the numbered floors to talk to me. Thank you."

"What's your name?" the guard asks, looking for the badge on Jerry's right hip.

He pulls his badge from its bungee lanyard and reads his names: "Dzherri, Jyotiranjan—"

"Your American name is fine," the guard interrupts. "Nice to meet you, Jerry."

Jerry cleans the sixty-seventh floor for a week. He breaks a lid every day and tells Charry that the bathroom fixtures are falling apart on the floor. Charry orders a new set of toilet paper holders, and just after New Year's Day 2076, Jerry has his reflective surface—panels of chrome lids lying on the floor of his studio apartment. When he turns on the light, he can see himself for the first time since entering The House.

His nose is thick and bell-shaped. His grin is wide and gap-toothed. His eyes are dark, moving clouds.

The reflective panels affect Jerry's dreams. He sees himself leading a conversation between groups of people. He sees himself talking on a headset in a glass office like he's on a conference call. He sees himself having one-on-one meetings with team members, reassuring them from behind a desk. Is he seeing who he was before he entered The House?

On January 5, Peter stands atop a chair in the kitchen and speaks to a gathering of twenty or so Americans. Peter says he knows that many of them are afraid that they will lose their jobs if they walk out on January 7th. He understands if they choose not to participate. He says that he expects to be let go, regardless of whether or not the walkout happens.

"I'm taking a stand for what's right," Peter says. "Ask yourself whose side you're on." He points in Jerry's direction. "Jerry tells me that no one talks to him on the numbered floors. Just because he's a rehabilitant. Isn't that right, Jerry?"

The Americans face him. He burns. What Peter is saying is not true anymore. The guard on the sixty-seventh floor spoke to him. Jerry wants to leave but doesn't want to appear to be fleeing.

"He's not even human to them," Peter says. "He just cleans their dirty squat holes. Doesn't he deserve better? Don't we all?"

Peter continues to spout on, but Jerry isn't listening. His fists are clenched. Peter has manipulated his words, shamed him to the rest of the workers. Jerry walks quickly toward the elevator that leads to the numbered floors. He gets his truck and wants to squeeze in another round of cleaning before going home.

Before Jerry can get his badge to the scanner, Charry calls his name. "Is it true?" he says. "You told Peter no one up there talks to you?"

"Well, yes, but—"

"Ostracism at Globe is unacceptable," Charry says, the cords in his neck thickening. "I know that the higher-ups have been discussing ways to ensure that more of the old American values are retained in our culture and—"

"I don't want to cause problems."

"Why didn't you come to me?" Charry says, his eyes probing Jerry's. "Why did you confide in Peter?"

"I didn't."

Charry's chin trembles. "You should have come to me," he says. "Without me, you wouldn't have been hired. I took care of you. I rewarded you. I gave you access. You and I have access. Long after Peter is a goner, we'll be here. That's what we can own."

The blinks come on like rain patter. Jerry's insides fall over and over. He can please neither Peter nor Charry. Complexity is the reward, he tells himself.

"You should have come to me," Charry repeats as he walks away.

After Jerry's rounds, he encounters Peter in the locker room.

"You misused my words," Jerry says.

Peter slams a boot on a bench and stretches. "I needed an anecdote to illustrate my ideas."

"You shouldn't have involved me."

Peter moves closer. His chest nearly bumps Jerry's shoulder. "Why?" he asks. "Because you love Globe so much?"

"Charry told me to keep my head down."

"That guy is just waiting for everyone else to get fired so he can be the king. But the king of what? The basement?"

Jerry's jaw clenches. "Every job is interconnected."

"Who cares? The point is: We deserve better."

"You've lost your will to compete."

Peter backs Jerry against his locker. "Do you know who you probably were? A degenerate. An addict. A criminal."

He goes on, his words warbling and rising in intensity and volume, but Jerry can't understand them. Jerry shuts his eyes and his eyelids are hot and he sees red. He draws his badge and holds it up to Peter.

Jerry feels a release in his chest as his hand empties. Peter puts the badge in his pants pocket.

"Thanks," he says. "We won't forget this."

It occurs to Jerry that he could warn Peter about the sixty-seventh floor. Jerry could say 1776 is futile. But Peter is still smirking as he exits the locker room.

Like he's already won.

Jerry calls in sick on January 7. The evening news covers a disturbance on Globe Island. Workers tried to open the windows on the second floor, only to find them locked. Security forces descended. Warnings were given. Shots were fired.

The body bags are stretchered out to red trucks. Medics trot gurneys out of the building. The covered corpses jiggle. The news shows the photographs of the basement employees. Twenty-five in all, including Peter.

Jerry turns off the television. His reflective panels go dark.

The next week is especially unproductive. Trauma counselors speak to the janitors for thirty minutes about coping skills. Because he's just a contractor, Jerry is the only employee not interviewed. He is thankful to be excluded, but some of the Americans suspect that Jerry was an accomplice because his badge was found on Peter's body.

Charry doesn't show up to the office. Rumor has it that he is under investigation. There is talk among both the employees and the management that there should be more mixing between national units, perhaps the occasional team-building event or lunch together. But no action items are taken, and no top-down initiatives are promised.

On a rainy day, two weeks after 1776, Jerry is summoned to The House. Inside the meeting booth, Jerry flips the switch on the audio box.

"I was concerned for you," Mentor says.

"I am safe."

"Did you know the workers?"

Jerry says he knew one.

"Did you sympathize with him?"

"No."

"I don't believe you, Jerry."

"I am telling the truth."

The box emits static and then quiets.

"Charry informed me that you were unhappy," Mentor says. "That you and Peter developed a relationship and you helped him. You gave him your badge. Without your badge, nothing would have happened."

Jerry's mouth is dry. Though what Charry described is not entirely true, there's nothing specifically untrue that Jerry can deny.

"I was being manipulated," he blurts. "I just wanted it to stop. I knew the sixty-seventh floor would do the stopping."

The box is silent.

"I was only trying to do right," Jerry says. "Peter didn't want to compete for his place in line."

More silence.

"Why did I enter The House?" Jerry asks. "What was my crime?"

"You don't want to know."

"I do."

"I'm giving you one more chance to say that you don't."

Jerry knows that Mentor does not want to answer because it means Jerry's treatment will have to be reinforced. But he remembers his bell-shaped nose, his wide and toothy grin, and his dead black eyes.

"I want to know who I really am."

"You are a janitor, Jerry," Mentor says. "Nothing more or less."

"I am an American."

Mentor snickers. "What does that even mean anymore?"

"I want to know who I was," Jerry says. "I deserve the opportunity."

Mentor sighs. "Unfortunate. You filled your role *perfectly*."

The booth door flies open. A pair of men wearing white awaits. "You worked for Globe in Los Angeles," Mentor says. "You led a walkout. You would not accept your place in line."

5

Ringleaders

In my class, Oscar is the ringleader. He's got short legs, shorter arms, and the barrel belly of a sturdy man's miniature. He carries himself with the confidence and self-satisfaction of a morally challenged authority figure: a crime organization don, a politician on the take, or a global investment bank executive—hypercompetitive and lawless like the people for which I used to work. Today, he's wearing soccer shorts, an Argentina jersey, and goalie gloves so rank with sweat that I can smell them as he passes my desk. As usual, he's brought some version of a game he'll cajole the other eight-year-olds into playing, and then he'll make fools of them. He holds a stack of paper demitasses—Three Cups and a Coin, the shell game. In the back of the classroom, he lays them mouth-down on his desk, then waits, cross-armed and smiling big. I ask the class to take out a sheet of paper and begin today's assignment: writing a letter to the President.

"Come on!" Oscar shouts at Ashanti, a black girl whose mother makes her flatten her hair every two weeks. She touches her head the way people repeatedly touch things that hurt.

"No way!" she says. "You're a cheater!"

"I'm not a cheater!" Oscar says. "I'm better!"

He hides a coin under the cup and commences shuffling.

Ashanti gradually drifts toward the game. Deshawn, a buck-toothed kid no one plays with because he's so quiet, follows her. A few others join, and soon, Oscar is surrounded, hollering, "Find the coin! Bet you don't know where it is!"

I should break his little game up, but just the thought of it exhausts me. A class of fifty is a lot for one teacher to handle, and this year, the district gave me a partner. So I wait for Ashley, who's explaining the assignment to one of the girls, to discipline Oscar.

I help LaShaundra because she's docile. Oscar's congregation is at six and counting.

"LaShaundra," I say. "Have you ever wanted to ask anything of the President?"

"My name is Karla." She points across the room at one of the other bespectacled black girls. "She's LaShaundra."

I look at LaShaundra and then at Karla. They look almost nothing alike. LaShaundra is light-skinned with curly tresses. Karla has cornrows. Don't judge. You try remembering the names of fifty new kids each year.

"Write," I tell Karla.

"Oscar!" Ashley scurries to the back of the room, where he is jumping on his seat like Rich Uncle Pennybags on speed. I catch Ashley's eye as she's ordering Oscar to sit down. I make an effort to appear appreciative that she's saved me, though I had no intention of taking any action.

I hope she never becomes like me.

Ashley's dark-haired and of some mysterious ethnicity. Two years out of Wellesley, new to San Francisco, she's all earnestness and enthusiasm. Her voice cracks like a wind instrument.

She comes to school wearing pencil skirts and crisp, collared blouses beneath cardigans, like she's off to a job interview after class.

Ashley and I talk, text, and lunch together. We find moments during the school day to look into each other's eyes like intimates. We're having a microaffair. Whenever I meet people her age, I'm surprised how appalled they are by certain transgressions but indifferent to others. Ashley was enraged when she heard that one of the faculty members was having an affair with another, but she has no opinion on issues like the global financial crisis and subsequent Great Recession, wealth inequality, or our forever war-related entrée into torture, citizen spying, and airborne death robots.

She loves children, feels very passionate about fighting to make their lives better despite the many, well-documented obstacles built into our public education system (or any institution not private for that matter). I advise her to never lose passion, never give up, and she seems to consider me worthy of such rosewater messages. What she doesn't appear to notice, however, is that recently, I'm finding it difficult to follow my own advice.

I've been teaching third grade for five years. For ten, I managed a sales support team at one of the big investment banks in New York before leaving during the heat of the financial crisis. We supported groups that sold credit default swaps. In corporate finance, we facilitated handshakes between rich folks, who were trading funds filled with other people's money, betting on both sides of the market. Like Oscar, we coerced them to play in a game that we rigged. Even after the world economy started crumbling in our hands, none of us worried about losing our jobs. "We'll be fine," my boss said. "We're massive." When I explained that I couldn't in good conscience do work that I felt was wrong and destructive to the disadvantaged, he chuckled and quipped, "Whaddaya gonna do? Teach?"

Soon after I quit, my wife Tina, who had been looking for a cardiology fellowship after completing her residency at Weill Cornell, landed a gig at UCSF, and we moved across the country.

Occasionally, I'll get gifts from the parents of former students who are now putting their younger ones through my class. Deshawn's mother brought me a slice of sweet potato pie last month and said that her oldest son Andre had gotten into one of the top private high schools in the area. I allowed myself to feel proud for a moment and then asked what Andre wanted to do when he grew up.

"He wants to go into finance, where you used to be," she said. "There, he doesn't have to struggle."

Tina was supportive when I decided to get my credential and teach for a fraction of what I used to earn. *Was supportive.* We get by on her salary. "You owe it to yourself to discover what you love," she said as if the words were foreign, as if she were trying to convince herself. Last week at my cousin's red egg and ginger party for their new baby, when my grandparents asked her how I was doing (they never believe me when I say I'm fine), Tina lied and told them I was planning a return to banking. Sometimes when you lie, you reveal your true desires. You reveal what's underneath, like when you shuffle the cups and inadvertently show the coin.

My grandmother calls my wife once a week to discuss their favorite topic: me. I can't hear what Grandma is saying, but I can imagine it well enough. Why don't I want to give them *great*-grandchildren? What's going on in my head? Why am I teaching? That's a hopeless, poor person's profession. Do something in life at which you have a chance to succeed. Let better, dumber people do the death march!

"I know, Grandma," Tina says in Mandarin. "You're right....Yes, we should be having children soon. We're so busy....Yes, I know adoption is not the real thing."

I'm lying on the couch, reading stories by Richard Yates.

Tina hangs up with a sigh.

"She's at me again, huh?" I say.

"She's at us," she says as she moves my feet, sits, and begins fingering the remote to find one of her shows—no doubt one with larger houses and lots of babies.

"Don't you think it's greedy for her to want great-grandchildren?" I ask.

"When you don't do what they want, it reflects badly on me as a wife."

Her snipe surprises, cuts. I'm careful not to react, not to escalate. I pretend to read. But I fail to suffer the silence and say, "Maybe I'm not turning out to be the man you married."

She's watching a show about million-dollar rooms that are all much larger than our apartment. Rooms paid for by sweatless bankers and other such men pedaling tandem bikes to Retire-at-Fifty-Five Town.

Tina flips to another show. Another home renovation. Another nursery.

"You don't even try," she says.

"It's about enjoying the journey," I say, attempting to inject levity into the conversation, the room, our lives.

"Yeah, well, you don't enjoy that, either?" Tina leaves the remote on my belly and gets up to go to bed.

Who can blame her for being supportive in the way that suggests that support is a wifely box one checks? When you withdraw money at the cash machine every week and there's half of what there used to be, being St. Wife isn't so easy. Tina's always been a pleaser. As a Chinese guy, I'm supposed to find it charming that she speaks perfect Shanghai-nese, goes out of her way to pour tea for elders at banquets, and gets enthusiastic about extended family trips to the homeland. She says she wouldn't mind if, after we have kids, we rented a house in the suburbs big enough for all four of our parents! Tina's perfect for them. She loves serving others, and more importantly, she loves being told she's great at serving others. We used to be great at serving each other. By the time we left Manhattan, we had eaten at least once at every Michelin-starred restaurant on the island and often made a point of relaying this fun fact to our friends.

Now I'm just one of many family members she serves, just as I'm one of many poorly paid, charred-to-a-husk teachers of children who have no desire to learn what we have to teach.

Playground time. Randall, a guest science teacher, will demonstrate how to blow large bubbles using a tub of soapy water and twine. Outside, it's sunny for the first time all summer, and Ashley and I move the kids from the classroom to the playground in a sinuous single file. There's a grass field surrounding the blacktop and a twenty-foot fence that would stop most in-shape adults, though last year, a first grader got so high up that we had to call the fire department to get him down. Oscar begins a headlong sprint around the playground, looping back toward the line to tag the arms of the kids he's chosen to join his Olympic relay.

"Oscar!" I say sharply. But he pays me no mind. Soon, he's got a train of kids doing laps. Ashley tries to block him, but Oscar just runs around her. The kids who aren't running are whooping like they're celebrating a successful coup d'état. Ashley and I exchange helpless, exasperated looks. Correction: I'm the one that looks helpless. She looks determined. Randall, the old science guy, stands on the grass, grimacing behind his eyeglasses at the sun and dangling an impotent rope in the suds bucket. He's been a teacher for decades. How has he not given up?

"All right, everyone!" he calls out. "Bubbles!"

Just like that, Oscar the Ringleader leads his troops right to Randall's bucket, and they sit cross-legged before Señor Science like they're at home watching Nickelodeon.

"How does he do that?" I ask Ashley, who sidles over to me, arms akimbo, looking in full command.

"Randall's got this now," she says. "All we have to do is keep them inside the fences."

At Ashley, I have no trouble smiling. She's wearing a lime-green blouse with a Peter Pan collar, dark jeans, and flats. Her clothes look way more expensive than she should be able to afford on her salary. I've noticed that about people her age. They keep up with the Joneses. Her teeth are perfect. I suspect that, as a product of miscegenation, she's genetically superior to me, and consequently I find her mildly intimidating. I don't know what the deal is with her thirteen-year-old boy voice, but life is a puzzle.

"How's the roommate?" I ask. Her roommate is in a contentious relationship. Asking about Ashley's personal life makes me feel young and hopeful.

"Ugh, I've resorted to hanging out at the corner bar until they're asleep," she says.

I wonder what would happen if Ashley and I had a drink together tonight while Tina's at the hospital. Would that violate the terms of our microaffair? You know what? Nothing would happen, because 1) I'm too old for the corner bars frequented by Ashley and her cohort and 2) I'm too lazy to deal with Tina's inevitable questions.

With his wands, Randall raises the twine from the bucket and slowly parts the loop while backpedaling. A large, rainbow-tinted bubble rises and swoops through the air. The kids ooh and ahh and run after the floating globule. Though I see this experiment every year, even I experience a certain sense of wonder at the bubble's size and trajectory. Randall makes another smaller one, and it bursts almost immediately.

"Why are some bubbles bigger than others? Why does one rise while others burst?" I ask Ashley.

She pulls out her phone, touches the screen a few times, and finds a website with information about bubble-related science projects. "Did you know that bubble skin is a thin layer of water sandwiched between two layers of soap molecules?"

"I had no idea." It's amazing how little one needs to know to teach.

"Can one of you get that other bucket?" Randall calls out to us. "We'll show them how to merge bubbles."

Ashley trots over to him. I feel smaller without my micromistress by my side. She makes a large bubble. It rises to meet Randall's, and together they form a giant one that draws more awed gasps from the children. I gasp as well—partly because I'm watching Ashley as she raises her arms and balances on the balls of one foot, trying to match the height of Randall's bubble. She looks like she's got the world at her fingertips, and it's the weight of a beach ball.

Today, Oscar's game is marbles, and in the back corner, he moves four desks so that the legs form an octagon—a makeshift arena. In it, he lines up the marbles so that the other students can take their crack at knocking them out. At the end of Oscar's game, these school property marbles will likely be lost because they'll be beneath the cupboards. Ashley writes today's vocabulary exercise on the chalkboard (is it pack of wolves, piece of wolves, group of wolves, or stick of wolves?).

She glances at Oscar, then me, and says, "Your turn."

"All right, break it up, Oscar," I say, approaching the gathering.

He pays no attention, of course. He kneels and flicks a marble, which clinks one in the line and knocks it beneath the cupboards as I predicted.

"Yes!" Oscar says, throwing gloved fists in the air as his followers cheer.

"We're going to start class now," I say. "You can play this game alone outside if you like."

"I don't want to play outside," he says. "I want to play in here!"

LeShaundra, Ashanti, Karla, Deshawn and others are huddled beneath the desks, waiting for me to go away. How will they keep track of who wins if the marbles get lost? Then I notice that Oscar is holding extra marbles in his left hand, ready to declare himself the winner no matter what happens.

I tell Oscar's followers to go back to their desks, and slowly they do.

"I win!" Oscar shouts, thrusting skyward the three marbles in his hand.

"You cheated," LeShaundra and I say together.

"He always cheats," Deshawn says.

"You're just jealous because I won!"

I move aside a desk, step into the octagon, and sweep the marbles with the side of my foot.

They roll beneath the cupboard like scurrying insects. "Game over," I say.

Oscar slaps a desk with a palm. "We don't need you!"

I feel a snapping behind my eyes. "We don't need you, either." My tone is flat, my jaw taut.

"In your desks, everybody," Ashley keens. "That means you, Oscar."

He does as Miss Ashley says, all the while staring at me with a gloating smile. He shakes his head.

"*Mandilón*," he says.

After school, Ashley and I have that drink. In a dark, moldy corner bar nearby aptly named Amnesia.

"That little fucker is the worst," I say.

"Jesus!" Ashley says. "He's just a kid."

"I'm joking." Half-joking. I'm not sure why Oscar irks me so. It's not like he's privileged.

His mother is on food stamps. (I glimpsed a booklet of

them in her purse last year at our parent-teacher conference.) She's convinced Oscar is going to play pro soccer someday. "We should probably have a conference with his mom."

"I mentioned it to her yesterday," Ashley says. "She says she has to work. I think she knows it's disciplinary."

"Avoidant parents," I say. "My favorite." I have avoidant parents. Immigrants, they returned to Asia just before the financial meltdown. Now they split time between high-rise condos in Singapore and Hong Kong. I don't miss them.

Ashley says her roommate has asked whether she'd mind if her boyfriend moved in. Against her better judgment, Ashley has agreed. I can't help but be a little disappointed; I figured she'd have as strong a handle on her personal life as she has in the classroom.

"I'm going to start looking for a place tonight," she says. "Problem is I can't afford to live alone." Ashley peers into the mouth of her beer. "At least you're married."

"You can be married and alone."

When Ashley's brow arches, it causes no forehead wrinkles. She drinks. With considerable thirst, I must add. Was I seeing things? I'm fifteen years older than Ashley. Today, she looks barely of age. She's too young to even be my friend on Facebook. I order another round.

"Do you speak any Spanish?" I ask.

"A little."

"What does *mandilón* mean?"

Ashley laughs. "Who called you that?"

"Oscar."

She laughs so hard she spits up beer. I dutifully hand her

napkins. After she gathers herself, she tells me that *mandilón* means a man who is whipped by his woman.

My face flushes. "That little fucker."

Ashley and I don't have just one drink, of course. Or two. Or even three. I believe we stop at four. I manage a brotherly hug when we separate, mainly because I'm a lightweight, and after that many beers, my eyes are spinning like slot machine reels. Lucky for me, our apartment is empty when I get home. Tina is still at the hospital. I try to read more Yates, but I can't focus, and I'm skimming for the love scenes like a teenaged boy. I try to find some sports to watch, but both DVR tuners are on Tina's home improvement shows. I give up and begin dozing upright on the couch, and I wake to the sound of the front door opening and Tina walking in, still wearing her scrubs.

"Looking sexy there," she says.

I lift my chin off my chest and curse the sight of my belly. I remind myself of Oscar. "How was your day?" I ask.

"Are you drunk?"

"I had a drink."

"So you had two or three."

"Tough day."

"Did you just get home?" Tina snaps a takeout menu off the refrigerator door and the cordless phone off its base.

"I was going to order dinner," I lie.

"Chinese OK?"

I fucking hate Chinese. I hate everything about being Chinese. "Sure," I say.

Mandilón, I hear Oscar say. *Mandilón, mandilón!*

"Do you want me to return to banking?" I blurt.

She holds up a finger as she orders spinach with preserved egg, the empress chicken, and bitter melon and sea cucumbers (a dish I hate, but my grandma says we must have it at least once a week to promote heart health, and Tina the Cardiologist can most certainly never say no to healthy hearts).

"Thank you," she says before hanging up. "What did you say?"

"Do you want me to return to banking?" I repeat. "Like you said at the red egg and ginger party."

Tina snickers. "You've been holding that in since the party?"

"So?"

"You've had at least four drinks."

"Stop avoiding."

She sits on a bar stool in the kitchen. She looks like she's behind a teacher's desk. She looks like what I look like to Oscar. "I want you to do what makes you happy," she says.

"I don't believe you."

"What more do I have to do to convince you?" she says. "I let you do whatever you want."

"You haven't been standing up for me to my family."

"Because you won't talk to them, and they don't want to talk to you because you're grunting one-word answers at them all the time," she says. "I have no clue why it's so difficult for you to figure out what you want. I thought men were supposed to be binary."

"And what do you want?" I say. "A house? A baby? A house baby?"

"Go ahead and joke," she says. "Fine, I do want a house and

a baby. Someday. Now you tell me what you want because I know it's not teaching."

"I'm trying to figure that out."

Tina sighs. "Why do you think your parents moved back to Asia?"

"Because they like it there better than the U.S."

"But why?"

I have no clue why. We've never been close. At some point, during my teenaged years, we began to look alien to each other, our cores impregnable, our motives mysterious.

"I'll tell you why," Tina says. "Because shopping makes them happy, and in Asia, they don't have to feel bad about being lucky and enjoying life."

"That's a simplification."

"That's what your grandma said just last week," Tina says.

"But if you asked my parents—"

"I did!" she says. "They called me yesterday and said the same thing. Some things in life are just that simple. I became a doctor for the money. I don't want to struggle when I'm older. If you want to make me feel bad about that, go ahead. But I never feel bad about what I have and what I want. The world doesn't care where your heart is. It only cares that you have one and it works. So decide and get on with it."

Ashley looks like she hasn't slept, and she's wearing a sleeveless blue dress and gladiator sandals like she just went to Sunday brunch with her girlfriends. When Oscar walks in, we both hang our heads.

"We should have just kept drinking," I say.

Ashley smirks. "My roommates (plural) were fighting all night."

"My wife and I had a long conversation about what I should do with my life."

"And?"

"I'm here today," I say. "So obviously I made the wrong decision."

She laughs. "My roommate thinks her boyfriend is still hung up on his ex because he always invites her to come along on their dates."

"That's because he's still hung up on his ex."

With shut eyes, Ashley pinches her nasion.

Oscar pulls out a stack of warped-edge papers from his backpack.

"What's that, Oscar?" I ask.

"This doesn't concern you," he says.

"Did you hear that line in a movie or something?"

Ashley pushes away from our desk, shoulders rounded. "My turn."

"No, I got it," I say, remembering what Tina said about the world not caring about my heart. Decide and move on. I finish writing today's math lesson on the board and head toward Ringleader. He's passing out these papers to the others, and they are laughing. A grinning Oscar hands me one.

It's a crude drawing of a dark-haired man lying on top of a dark-haired woman. The title of this masterpiece is "Miss Ashley and *Mandilón*." The drawing doesn't portray anything I haven't fantasized about already. But I crumple it and begin collecting the many variations (an eight-year-old's Kama Sutra) from the students, and I crumple those as well. I fling one balled-up flyer at a time at Oscar, bouncing them off his belly and face, and while he's distracted, I confiscate the box.

Oscar charges and shoves me in the groin. "Give it back!" he growls as I tower over him. He begins to slap my belly, and I'm chagrined at how my paunch meat ripples and shudders, how I've let myself go. The class laughs at this game Ringleader and I are playing.

"In your desk, Oscar!" Ashley shouts.

He reaches for the box, which I hold up and out of his grasp.

"You and Miss Ashley are going to get married!"

"I'm already married."

Oscar slaps me again on the belly. "You're dee-vorce," he begins to sing repeatedly, pivoting his head left and right while he persists in slapping me like we're convivial frat brothers.

I throw the box across the room and grab his hands hard. "You little fucker," I hiss.

The boy's face darkens with fear. I've grabbed him harder than intended. I'm reminded that Oscar has his own story, his own weight, his own reasons (though he may not be aware of them yet) for his actions. One day, he might even develop his own conscience. Simultaneously, I release and push him toward his seat. I walk back toward Ashley, feeling fifty pairs of eyes upon me as she starts the day's first lesson.

After class, instead of sitting behind my desk, I choose a student's. As I slide into the too-small chair, I want to say many things to Ashley. I hope my flagging faith in teaching isn't rubbing off on her. I don't want to be a ringleader.

"That's going to get back to the administration," I say as Ashley erases the chalkboard.

She offers me a piteous look. "For the record, I didn't see what happened."

"My wife thinks I feel bad about too many things."

"Does she ask about you and me?"

"No."

She continues erasing the board, more slowly than before.

"I want to quit." Her voice squeaks on the word "quit."

"Why?"

"I want my own place," she says. "I love the kids, but I don't make enough money. All my friends make more money. I'm tired of not being able to afford to go to brunch or happy hour with my friends."

Ashley sits beside me, also in a student's desk, and we face the blank chalkboard. I feel something inside me warm, and the deck of my world cantilevers, and I'm backsliding. I take her hand. She doesn't seem to mind.

"Does your wife have any suggestions about what you should do with your life?"

"The Chinese are the most suggestive of ethnicities," I say. "She wants me to go back to banking so we can more easily afford a kid and a house."

"Is that what you want?"

"I only seem to know what I don't want."

Ashley lets my hand go and adjusts her bangs so that they hang over her eyes like a modern rock singer from the nineties, bored with the melodies she's singing. This look is so attractive that I can feel my heart pulsing from my chest to my back. If I told Ashley why she looked so attractive, she'd have no clue what I was talking about because she was born in the nineties.

"Miss Ashley?" It's Deshawn in the doorway.

"Where's your mom?" she asks.

"She's late," he says. "Someone stole my lunch money check out of my backpack."

Ashley emits an outsized oh-no. "Was it Oscar?"

Deshawn shakes his head. "It was one of the fourth graders. Oscar tried to stop them." Ashley and I exchange surprised looks. Deshawn starts to cry. The kid is a worrier. He's already got stray gray hairs and creases between his eyes. He holds his elbows like he's cold.

"All right, why don't we go outside, and you can show me what happened?" Ashley says, getting up. She looks at me, her jaw firm, and says, "Wait for me?"

I nod, unsettled and titillated by her ask. I force a smile for Deshawn. I want to hug him and tell him everything will be fine, but I know I shouldn't lie.

It's been nineteen months since that afternoon. I didn't wait for Ashley. While she was with Deshawn, I marched to the principal's office and told him what I did to Oscar. I expressed contrition. I said he didn't have to contemplate my punishment, because I was resigning. I was thanked for my candor.

I'm thinking about Ashley because there's a new analyst on my team who reminds me of her. Smart, enthusiastic, just out of college, mature for her age, very poised in front of senior management. My vice president, a stout middle-aged man with an Oscaresque belly, a wife, four kids, and a very large house that's an hour and a half away by train, has already remarked that he'd very much like to fuck her. That's right,

I'm back in Lower Manhattan. Oscar was correct. I am a *mandilón*. My woman is a big bank.

Ashley finished out the semester before she quit too. She's now at Harvard getting a Master's in Education. In her last email to me, she wrote that "now that I've experienced the challenges of teaching at a public school, I want to one day become a district superintendent where I can facilitate true change." I couldn't help but wonder whether she had cut and pasted that from her admissions essay. My foray into teaching gives me a strange medallion of worldly credibility among coworkers, some of whom treat me as if I've just emerged unscathed from a safari that ended murderously. Tina and I got divorced.

The new analyst is about to come into my office for her first one-on-one. I'm going to try to guide her on the right path and quietly suggest that she avoids ringleaders like my boss. But I can't make decisions for her, and I've already proven to be a poor teacher. What I will say is that she should never lose passion, never give up, and at this company—one of the world's oldest and most revered financial institutions—happiness can be elusive, but it is something you make, like a giant bubble.

6

Matador Meltdowns

The morning after Rajeev and I first slept together, we shuffled silently across the Great Bridge over the Charles River. We didn't touch. We didn't look at each other. I walked a few steps behind him. Upon arriving at our second-year Leadership and Corporate Accountability (LCA) class, we split to opposite sides of the room, took our seats in the terraced semicircles, and withdrew our name placards. This was the plan I had asked Rajeev to execute when we left my apartment. I didn't want to give our classmates reason to chatter.

That was the day Professor Fernando Aguilar entered wearing a matador costume: dark cape, sparkling gold jacket, red waistcoat, and stretch pants over bony legs. Wielding a play sword, Professor Aguilar stepped in front of the podium—straight-backed with thighs pressed together—and declared that we, the students, had chosen to attend business school to participate in a bloody, metaphorical bullfight.

"The bull is not you!" he proclaimed. "The bull is everyone else. You and I pretend that we're keenly sensitive to the position the bull is in, but we are not. We pretend that as the next generation of business leaders, we want to make the world a better place. But we are only here to become the matador! One day, we will watch the bull bleed to a slow and painful death."

Professor Aguilar unclasped his cape and waved it back and

forth before thrusting the plastic blade through the air, crying out in exertion. Then he re-clasped the cape, sheathed the sword, and stomped out of the room, the red fabric flaring up and down like market caps in a flash crash.

The class snickered. Was Aguilar trying to be funny? Was he coming back?

Rajeev stared at me from across the room. I shouldn't have invited him over last night. Too much wine. That last tipple of Fernet. His cologne, after a long night out, had smelled of warm pies.

The thirty of us sat for several minutes, some murmuring with friends, others flipping through the case study booklet we had been scheduled to discuss: Governing Inamura Electronics Corporation. But Professor Aguilar did not return. Not that day. Not ever. We later heard that he had gone straight to the Dean's office to resign.

Once it became clear that class was over, I exited posthaste. Rajeev called out to me as I fled. He pronounced my name "Ahhhn," thinking he was being cute. When it was just the two of us, I found him amusing. But in front of everyone, his call felt territorial. I turned and asked what he wanted.

His lopsided grin disintegrated. I returned a few hellos from classmates and tried not to look at anyone long enough to encourage small talk.

"What just happened?" Rajeev asked.

I knew he was referring to Professor Matador, but I couldn't help thinking about the dawn-hour scramble into my bathroom, where, behind locked doors, I cowered on the toilet while Rajeev slept. What had I done? I just wanted to finish my MBA and get out of this place. I had no desire to get close to these matadors-in-training.

"I don't know," I said. "But it feels like an omen."

Crisp, fall Cambridge morning. The sun was out, and the surface of the Charles resembled gold leaf. Unclear who'd teach the class going forward, I was on my way to Baker Library to meet my LCA group, which consisted of:

Rajeev, a former venture capitalist.

Dell, who had spent the last five years as a surgeon in Belize.

Lindsey, who had hit it rich with an Internet company and was now completing an MBA as a hobby.

And then there was me, the former Chief Operating Officer of a five-employee nonprofit that raised money for autism research. I had no idea how I'd gotten into the best MBA program in the country. Perhaps I filled its quota for non-profiteers.

I spotted my group lounging in mocha-colored exposition chairs in the checkered-tiled common area. Lindsey sat bow-backed with her laptop balanced on crossed, pants-suited thighs. Dell was conscientiously finger-molesting his phone. Rajeev eyed me as if he'd been waiting for my arrival. We had, against my better judgment, slept together again. We had been at the same happy hour at Grendel's, and we had, yet a-fucking-gain, been the last ones out. I had to admit, he was handsome. He had the narrow waist and significant shoulders of a comic-book hero. In my bed, I vaguely recalled him slur-ring that he was past meaningless encounters and ready to set-tle down. I chuckled in response. When he asked what was funny, I pretended I was asleep.

To my horror, in front of everyone, Rajeev greeted me with a toothy-beamed hug and again called me "Ahhhn."

I practically dove into the seat between Lindsey and Dell and fixed my gaze on that morning's *The Wall Street Journal* on the round table. "Lehman Files for Bankruptcy, Merrill Sold, AIG Seeks Cash," the headline read.

"We should just stop showing up," said Lindsey. "It's not like LCA is a real class like finance."

"Leadership and Corporate Accountability is fairly useless," Rajeev said. "If you were not already a competent leader, you would not have been accepted into Harvard."

I felt a twinge of envy that Rajeev would agree with Lindsey. Did he like stocky girls with bad skin? I shouldn't have cared, shouldn't have been such a bitch, but hey, like Rajeev said: Accountability is fairly useless.

"Maybe Aguilar wasn't feeling the love," Dell said, making a big show of rubbing his thumb across the pads of his fingers.

Dell was a balding, perpetually sweaty fellow with the largest hands I'd ever seen. Hard to believe he had once been a surgeon. A scalpel must have looked like a toothpick in those kielbasa-like fingers. He was the fiftieth or sixtieth business student I'd met who found a way to equate love with compensation.

"What was Aguilar trying to say, anyway?" Rajeev said. "A bull is a man? A man is a bull?"

Lindsey adjusted her dark-rimmed glasses and squinted at the glowing PowerPoint presentation on her laptop screen. "Somebody get him a Kleenex."

"Anne called it an omen; isn't that right, Anne?" Rajeev's amber eyes were wide, searching, expectant.

Dell and Lindsey turned heads like interrupted birds in a wildlife preserve; I composed a smile. I missed the West Coast, my mom, my friends, my work. I wasn't made like these people.

"I don't know what I called it," I said. "I don't know anything."

While most of my fellow students planned to get winter internships at huge corporations to bolster their resumes and professional networks, I planned to go home to Vallejo, California. The previous summer, I had interned at Bain and Company in Boston; that was a disaster. In an office of hundreds, I was one of eight women, and they were bigger assholes than the guys, who were all massive ones. There was something anachronistic about people wearing business suits in floor-to-ceiling glass-walled offices staring at spreadsheets and printing out reams and reams of paper drenched in color toner, all to be bindered or VeloBound and read by middle-aged white male execs. The office had a culture in which saying the word "homosexual" was funny in just about any context, and you could refer to a female colleague's endowment as "tits." And the women spent every day from 3 PM to 4 PM sitting in black leather chairs in the lobby, Starbucks tall cups in hand, gossiping like a sewing coterie about which of their male coworkers was "cutest." In exchange for enduring this horrorshow, if I wanted, I could now step off to other management consulting firms that made as much money in twenty minutes as my old nonprofit made annually.

I hadn't been back to the West Coast since last Christmas. There, the worlds of my loved ones weren't just failing to grow—they were shrinking. For decades, my mom worked as a croupier at a Chinese casino and now lived in a RV park at the edge of acres and acres of fancy wineries and vacation homes the size of government buildings. Recently, her glaucoma had become so bad that she was forced to stop working. My best friend Carrie, pregnant with twins, lost her house because she and her husband had trapped themselves in a bad adjustable-rate mortgage. She was an office assistant and he was a teacher. It used to be that in their chosen professions, they were playing in a financial junior varsity that provided a modest level of long-term security. These days, they were playing a different game entirely, one with high risks and few rewards.

At Harvard, we didn't talk about people like my mom or Carrie. We talked about macroeconomic growth, making corporates more efficient, and most importantly, maximizing profits.

When I got my acceptance letter, I was excited. The nonprofit was teetering on bankruptcy's brink. I had been there too long; I wasn't learning anymore. Increasingly, we were reliant on the generosity of the very rich. When I started ten years before, we had a steady pipeline of smaller donations from people of every economic background. By the time I left, we spent most of our time on massive grant applications that had nine-to-twelve-month close cycles. Even if we overcame the long odds to score these grants, we wouldn't see a dime for years. I worked hard on the B-school apps, paid thousands to have my essays professionally edited, and took three GMAT prep classes. It would have taken Carrie and her husband seven years to gross the amount I borrowed to pay the tuition. I popped champagne (the cheap stuff) when I got in. I looked forward to communing with like-minded, entrepreneurial problem-solvers—some of the smartest in the world. But then I moved to Cambridge and discovered that B-school was far different than expected.

Harvard was an Everest that students felt they had earned, and once they arrived, it was a resort oasis for the already successful and well-rewarded, people for whom failure was either something they watched on television or talked about as an exception in their well-diversified portfolio of successes of all sizes and shapes. Rajeev, for instance, tried to hide his privileged background with his rakish, affable charm or the occasional well-placed reference to a not-that-obscure rock band, or some long-forgotten indolent backpacking adventure. He might even have truly seen himself as an everyman, but he couldn't hide his cobalt-blazered time on Sand Hill Road where he worked as an investment banker before founding his own VC that incubated dozens of early-stage startups, the most successful of which was an emojis-only forum site that sold for a whopping two billion dollars. He couldn't hide his midnight-blue BMW convertible in the campus parking lot or his twice-daily skincare regimen that involved his spending a thousand dollars a year at Sephora. His family was replete with doctors, lawyers, and bankers. His friends thought little of dropping five figures on weekend trips to Las Vegas or St. Thomas. The first time I met Rajeev was at the Meet and Greet Happy Hour arranged by the university. Without any prompting, he told me his family hailed from an upper caste in India, and one of the keys to thriving there was the ability to become comfortable with one's inherent superiority to lower castes. "In America, people don't like this idea of being better than someone who has less," he said. "But the fact is: you are better, by circumstance, by luck, by evolution, and quite possibly by genetics. You are better because you are educated. Because you will have a degree from Harvard. Spend a day in Mumbai among the beggars, the solicitors, and the maimed, and you will understand what I am telling you."

And there I was, continuing to sleep with Rajeev and his betterness. A very loud part of me was disgusted both with his gentried qualities and with myself for finding those qualities intriguing in ways I couldn't articulate.

Rajeev made himself at home on my couch. I went through the week-old pile of mail on my dining table.

"You've been acting strange," he said.

"I don't want everyone to know we're hooking up."

"Hooking up?" he said, open-groined, his left kneecap in hand. "Is that what this is?"

"Yes."

"I think you're beautiful."

"You don't know me."

Rajeev tilted his head and stared into the space between us. "I've had a crush on you since that first happy hour," he said. "I was very upset when you left early. But then we were together in Marketing—"

"Stop," I said, cradling the mail and sitting on the edge of the couch beside him.

Rajeev scooted close enough to make me spill half the envelopes. He wrapped a heavy arm around me. There it was, again. His warmth. His pie-smell.

"What do you need, Anne?" he asked, his face close to

mine. He did not twist and tease my name this time. I couldn't feel his breath. He was holding it. For me.

I kissed his purple lips, like he was exactly who I'd always wanted.

The Dean announced that our LCA class, for the remainder of the semester, would be taught by Professor Goodman, who also taught TEM (The Entrepreneurial Manager). The Dean apologized for Professor Aguilar's outburst and assured us that such outbursts would never happen again. She explained that a recent internal investigation uncovered that Professor Aguilar had been having psychological issues that she wasn't free to discuss.

"Here, we take the quality of your education very seriously because we are training tomorrow's leaders," the Dean said, reading a prepared statement through seemingly immovable bangs. "If you have any further concerns about this incident, please do not hesitate to email me."

She pivoted on her heel—as Professor Aguilar had—and marched out of the classroom.

"*Andalé*," Dell, who was sitting next to me, whispered in my ear with a smirk.

I glanced across the room at Rajeev to see if he'd notice that Dell, from a distance, might appear to be flirting with me. But Rajeev was smiling and chattering with that meathead Elmore Frednar. Yes, of the travel guide Frednar's. Yes, Rajeev and I had slept together again.

Afterward, he'd even said that he loved me.

"Don't worry, I don't expect you to respond in kind," he'd

said. "I want to show you that you can trust me." After a pause, he added: "I am an open kimono."

I cackled. Rajeev often spoke in business clichés. "I'm surprised you haven't called me a Chinese menu."

Rajeev blinked twice with his abnormally long lashes and rolled over, leaving me with his broad, woolly back.

Professor Goodman entered the class. He wore a black T-shirt that had evidently been washed as many times as there were dollars in the national debt counter. His jeans were too short for his alligator-skin boots. He said that many of us knew him already (which was true), and then he proceeded to list his lengthy credentials, which included various positions at just about every large Internet brand. But we all knew where he'd made the majority of his money. He sold a company that manufactured change machines for strip clubs. When a patron exchanged ten dollars, the machine returned nine one-dollar bills. At the end of the night, when the stripper exchanged eleven one-dollar bills, she would receive ten dollars. Most of both dollars went to Goodman's company as a convenience fee.

"I don't know anything about Corporate Governance," he quipped. "If one of my companies got big enough to be *governed*, I sold that sucker as soon as possible."

The class laughed, and it seemed all had returned to normal. We huddled in our groups to discuss the Inamura case. Inamura Electronics Corporation was a publicly traded company that, thanks to changes to the Japanese commercial code, faced a choice between keeping its current corporate governance model or adopting a U.S. one, which stressed management's fiduciary responsibility to shareholders. The CEO of

Inamura implemented the U.S. model but did so in a uniquely Japanese way, and we were to evaluate how well his model worked and how cross-cultural issues affected its implementation. Lindsey was very vocal that had the U.S. model been implemented as intended by its creators, the company would have produced more wealth for its shareholders. Rajeev agreed that the traditional Japanese model of being transparent to a broader set of stakeholders, including the company's employees and the local communities in which the company operated, was onerous and destined to become obsolete. Dell wondered if any governance model could truly satisfy every stakeholder. Rajeev requested my opinion.

"The employees might be the most important stakeholders of all," I said.

"I do not believe that is the central question of the case," Rajeev said.

"I don't know what you want from me," I snapped.

Rajeev flinched before exchanging a grin with Dell that bordered on insidious. "I agree that there are many, many stakeholders," Rajeev said.

Judging by Dell's befuddled, drippy-eyed look, he wasn't listening.

Lindsey appeared ready to gore me. "You can't please every stakeholder," she said. "Not if you want to generate wealth. Everyone wants wealth, but only a few can actually be wealthy. Wealth is not just a metaphor. It's measurable."

"Check it out." Dell nodded down at the abandoned podium where Professor Goodman was supposed to be. Instead he was outside the class, beyond the open doors, cell phone pressed to his ear and smiling.

"Why didn't I think of his idea?" Dell said.

Rajeev crumpled in his seat, shaking his head. "Such a great idea."

"Why?" I asked. "It's just a money-making scheme that literally adds no value to society. It doesn't help a single person."

My groupmates stared at me. Dell kept shaking his head at Goodman, whose hand was rubbing his belly beneath his T-shirt. Lindsey stared at Rajeev with greedy, ring-hawking eyes. I looked down at our casebook, the text blurring.

"It helps him," Rajeev said. "Isn't that why we're here?"

Rajeev's arms stretched across the back of my couch again. His phone was in his lap and white headphones plugged his ears as he told his friend in California that with his connections, he could get five million dollars of seed funding in five minutes.

"Just come up with the idea," he said, like that was even easier than raising the five million.

I was at the dining table, trying to write this paper on Inamura, trying not to calculate the mind-boggling cost of Rajeev's running outfit that included a shirt made of a trademarked wicking fabric and neon blue and orange shoes named The Wave Prophecy.

"I'm at my girlfriend's place," Rajeev said.

Cringing, I went out to the porch to call my mother.

"My Anne." The way she said my name made me smile.

"Is it sunny there?"

"Every day looks the same to me," she said cheerfully. She didn't mean to refer to her glaucoma. She was a person who always saw the world as iridescent.

"The days seem to be getting worse here," I said.

"Oh Annie, you think too much," she said. "I'm so proud. My girl is at the best school! I tell everyone you're at Harvard! I will hang your degree in the living room."

Her pride filled my chest, and I wished it didn't. "How do you feel?"

She sighed. "Same same."

The door opened and Rajeev joined me on the porch. "What are you doing out here?" he said, even though it was obvious I was on the phone.

"Who's that?" my mother asked.

"A friend," I said.

"What's his name?"

Rajeev put his arm around me and waited. I said his name. "Tell him hi."

"My mom says hi."

Rajeev swelled with pleasure. "Hi, Mom!"

My cheeks burned. I told my mother I'd call her later. Before she let me go, she said I should try to be happier.

On television, Paulson and Bernanke announced their plan to buy hundreds of millions of dollars of Wall Street's bad debt. They somehow managed to look both baffled and conspiratorial, exactly how our Dean looked after the Aguilar incident, and how Professor Goodman looked pretty much all the time. I left for my 11 AM class.

Crisp, fall Cambridge morning. The sun was out, and the crew boys were splitting the Charles. When I got to Baker Library, Lindsey, Dell, and five or six others were standing and watching Rajeev. His back was to me and his thighs were pressed together, hands on hips. He faked removing a cape, unsheathing a sword, and killing a bull.

"The bull is man!" he shouted. "We are killing the bull!"

A torrent of laughter. Rajeev caught my eye and winked. I disappeared behind the crowd. Dell appeared at my side.

"What do you think of his matador?"

I rolled my eyes.

"That's the look my ex-wife used to give me," he said, laughing loudly.

I resisted the urge to hit Big Dell. I didn't know him well enough. I asked where he was from.

"Evansville, Illinois," he answered quietly, shifting in his Birkenstocks, hands stuffed in gigantic cargo shorts. "My family owns a chain of deep-dish pizza restaurants."

Rajeev and the crowd drifted further from Dell and me. Another student was now trying to emulate a matador. Rajeev attempted his impression again, this time with greater exaggeration. This version included galloping and thigh-slapping, drawing whoops and applause.

"I want to be the bull," Lindsey cooed.

"I could really go for a burger right now," Dell said.

"Let's go."

"Don't we have class?"

I began walking. "Are you coming?"

We ditched the bullfight and walked off campus, back across the Charles toward Harvard Square. In the short distance between the library and the river, Dell worked up a good sweat, blotching his maroon Michigan T-shirt. He said he liked the burgers at John Harvard's.

"He's crazy about you, you know that, right?" Dell said,

hands on his laboring hips, tongue lolling from an open mouth.

I sighed. "I know. But I just don't feel right."

"You don't like it here," he said. "And he's totally in his element."

"I feel like a fraud," I said. "I feel like we're all frauds."

"Hey!" Dell said. "Speak for yourself."

I apologized. "I know it's all me."

"I feel that way sometimes, too," Dell said. "But you can feel guilty about being here, or you can use it to your advantage."

"I just think Rajeev would be better off with someone more like him."

"You mean someone more like Lindsey?"

I noticed I'd started sweating, too. I shrugged. "Why not someone like her instead?

Dell looked at me as if I'd asked a stupid question. The longer he went without answering, the more I realized he didn't know, either. I was never someone who went out of my way to attract men. They were a mystery to me. I vaguely knew that if I did my hair a certain way or put on makeup or showed more skin, men saw me differently. But I considered myself plain. My longest relationship had lasted ten months.

"No one has ever treated me as well as Rajeev," I admitted.

"You should be talking about this with him."

"He and I don't do enough talking."

"Wow, I didn't need to know that."

I gave Dell a good smack on the arm.

Rajeev was making lentil soup in one of my pots. My mother and I moved around a lot when I was younger, and our kitchenware was often all we took from place to place. We didn't get attached to our other possessions, like the flimsy fold-up chairs or the threadbare linens. But our pots, pans, and silverware? We *groomed and doted* on them. Mom saved to buy the best brands.

I tried not to be irritated that we never hung out at Rajeev's place. I was always the host, and he always used my stuff. He treated my apartment like a hotel room. One night, he even left a towel on the bathroom floor. When I pointed out that I wasn't his maid, he claimed that the towel had fallen from the wall rod—but if it had, the towel had miraculously flown to the center of the room.

"I think I have an in on a shadow internship this winter," Rajeev said, lidding my Le Creuset.

"That's great," I said, skimming *The New York Times* front page. A photo showed Paulson pumping the president's hand. They looked ready to complete a multi-step fraternal shake.

"PWC in San Francisco," Rajeev said. "Your mom lives nearby, correct? Would you like to come along?"

I first thought of having Cambridge to myself for a month. Then I felt a pang that I would indeed miss Rajeev. I said maybe.

"What are you planning this winter?" he asked.

"I haven't thought about it," I lied.

"Are you thinking east? West? Abroad?"

"Yes."

Rajeev left the stove and side-saddled the dining room chair, crossing his long legs. "Anne," he said. "You are very secretive. I feel I must point this out to you."

My jaw clenched. "I'm sorry you feel that way."

"My family will be visiting next month," he said. "I would like you to meet them."

"OK."

"But you would not like me to meet your family?"

"No."

"Are you not aware that this hurts my feelings?"

"I'm sorry," I said. "I really am. I just can't—"

"Where did you go with Dell?"

Warmth commenced its silent strangle. "He was hungry. You were too busy breakdancing or whatever."

"We were having fun in business school," Rajeev said. "You should try it sometime."

"It's fun to watch the bull bleed."

Rajeev shook his head at the heavens.

"Everyone here is always the solution, never the problem," I went on. "But look what's happening in the world. That's the fault of people like us." Like you, I wanted to say.

The soup began to boil over. "I feel like the girl in this relationship," Rajeev said.

My face flushed with rage. "This is not a relationship."

Rajeev killed the stove and we listened to spilled broth sizzling on the range.

"Finally," he said, "you've given me an answer."

Then he left.

I dumped the lentils and washed my pot out twice. I knew I shouldn't have been so harsh. Truth was, I didn't know Rajeev well enough to have any clue whether he had gone through his own hardships. I felt a great opening inside me, and things were falling out, like I was a gutted purse. I tried to stop crying, but parts of me kept quaking, and eventually I gave up and let the loneliness and alienation and homesickness fall and aired the voids I wouldn't let Rajeev fill.

After I composed myself, I felt strangely light, free even. My skin was moist, like I had melted and begun hardening again. I walked out toward Harvard Square. The night was unseasonably warm and humid. I crossed Mass Ave. and entered Leo's Place, a mostly empty diner across from the T stop. I sat in a booth and ordered a cheeseburger. Leo's Place was a sad substitute for my favorite greasy diners back home, nothing like Bella's, where my mother used to work her second job and where Carrie and I used to get late-night waffles. We went there well into our adulthoods.

There were only three other patrons in Leo's. A Chinese couple studied together, books open, computers out. Two booths over was Professor Aguilar. He cupped a mug with both palms and appeared to be staring inside himself. I tried to catch his attention, but he ignored me. I decided to approach him.

"Professor Aguilar?"

"Please, call me Fernando." He invited me to sit. "Were you in one of my classes?"

I told him I was.

"I was having a very bad week," he said. "As it turned out, so was Merrill, so was Lehman, and so was America."

He sounded like he was mocking a cable news talking head. In class, his hair was slicked back. Here, it looked dry and brittle and flecked with silver, and the sclera of his eyes were purplish.

"What will you do now?" I asked.

A dimple rose on a side of his face. "I will be fine. You and I are the matadors, remember? That's why students pay to come here: to be forever fine." He scrutinized his lifeless coffee.

"You know what? I've always loved diner coffee."

"Me, too."

"The fancy stuff is way too strong for me," he said. "Maybe I should have used that metaphor instead. I should have come into class with a coffee pot. 'The wealthy are like artisanal coffee. Too strong!'"

We laughed dumbly. He asked for a refill from the waitress without bothering to look her in the face. I'd seen that indifferent glance a million times growing up when I watched my mother on the job—the waitress might as well have been a vending machine. She returned with Aguilar's bill on a plastic tray, and he plunked a folded twenty on the table. He pressed it flat, admiring it.

"I want to quit, too," I said. "I'm not sure it's right to be here."

"I didn't quit, Miss," he said. "I was fired. Several students complained. Why do you think I put on that foolish outfit to begin with? It was part of a lesson. I wanted you to think about how you'd respond to a protestor using leadership and corporate accountability principles."

"We pretended it wasn't happening," I said.

Professor Aguilar smirked. "If I were a protester that confronted you on the street, what would you say?"

I considered my answer for some time. "I'd tell you that when I was in B-school, no one took corporate accountability seriously, and that it was an easy, soft class compared to finance. And that's why we're here."

The professor nodded. "Not bad. But if I can't quit, you shouldn't have the luxury to do so, either."

We pulled into the parking lot at Bella's in Carrie's used Chevy Uplander, a General Motors minivan. It was a chilly December morning, the day after the U.S. Treasury Department announced a seventeen-billion-dollar taxpayer bailout of G.M. and Chrysler, about two weeks before the Fed announced it would bail out Fannie Mae and Freddie Mac.

Inside the restaurant, my near-blind mother braced herself against Rajeev's forearm as she slid into the booth. Rajeev sat by the window across from her, and my mom couldn't take her clouded eyes off him, couldn't stop beaming. I sat across from Carrie, who gently rocked her twin stroller with her three-month-old boys, Rob and Darren, whose expressions were pensive, concerned, if you looked at them long enough, even disapproving. Carrie and her family of four had put all their things into storage and were staying in a mobile home in the same RV park as my mother while they searched for a landlord who would take Section 8 applicants. She looked suddenly a decade older to me. She had a stack of forehead creases I didn't remember, and she moved with an economy of motion of someone now accustomed to completing every task using the least possible amount of time and energy possible. No gossipy coffee klatches in Carrie's world. Certainly no weeks off like Rajeev had just had—he had flown into the Bay Area directly from Dubai, where he had enjoyed a four-day bachelor's party with his buddies.

"So, Rajeev," Carrie said, "why Anne?"

A slow smile bloomed on his face. He clasped my hand

under the table. "Can I tell you how glad I am you asked?" he said. "I've been waiting to give all of you my elevator pitch."

"I'm trying to get him to stop speaking in business clichés," I said.

Rajeev blushed. "I'm trying to be better," he said. "Anne is helping me increase my visibility into what is really happening to people. We must level-set with each other as much as possible in this very difficult time." He winced, realizing that he was again sounding like a corporate shill. "I'm sorry."

My mom, Carrie, and I laughed.

I ran my fingers through his thick dark locks. Rajeev tilted his head toward mine, smiling at my family. I felt full, almost happy like my mother said I should try to be. I'm trying, too, I wanted to say.

I lay awake, staring out our bedroom window at the old elm tree in the park across the street. Rajeev is asleep beside me. We graduate today. This summer, we're moving back to San Francisco. Rajeev will be working for Google in product development. I'll be working at UC Berkeley, heading the alumni fundraising department. The worst of the meltdown seems to be over.

Rajeev and I often joke that we're just taking a break before the next one.

Will we try to be better? Or will we just pretend this never happened?

He turns over, strokes my face, my hair. Kisses my cheek. I push him away and get out of bed. I look down upon my smiling bull. He gets on all fours on the mattress, threatening to pounce. I press my thighs together, straighten my back, and stiffen my chin. As he begins to tell me again that he loves me, I unclasp an imaginary cape and wait for his charge.

7

Caroline's Notes

Caroline sat across from me in the cantina and told me she'd been writing suicide notes on resume paper with a fountain pen for months.

I hoped she was lying. Or telling an unfunny joke. But when she listed the places in the city she imagined offing herself (the Little Mermaid for the view, Nyhavn for the crowds, Christiania for the ideals, and so on), I realized she was quite serious.

"If you get to know me better, you might receive one in the post," she said with a smile.

I didn't know her at all. She was just a classmate, a fellow American, Chinese like me. There weren't many Asians at the university (or in the country, for that matter).

"Why are you telling me this?" I asked.

She pulled out a half-pack of Prince's from the breast pocket of her jacket, drew two cigarettes, and handed me one. "I had a feeling you'd understand," she said.

I shut the book I'd been reading (Saul Bellow's *Dangling Man*) and let her light me. She was plain at best, unattractive at worst. She had yellow crooked teeth, mousy chapped lips, and an outbreak of acne on her left cheek that was angry with whiteheads. Her dark hair was straight and shoulder-length; her ears revealed themselves. She wore tight black jeans that made her bottom half look big. She knew I was a smoker, though we'd spoken only once—a few weeks ago. Caroline and I were in the same American Lit of the 1940s and 1950s class taught by Professor Lebowitz. The syllabus consisted only of American Jewish male authors, many of whom resembled the professor in appearance.

"How do you like the Bellow?" Caroline asked.

I squinted at the bug-eyed, gape-mouthed, balding head-shot on the back cover. "Did everyone writing novels in America fifty years ago look like Professor Lebowitz?"

Caroline half-smiled. "People can't get beyond themselves, can they?" she said.

I didn't know what to say to that one. The cantina rattled and buzzed. We were behind a plate rack, the unofficial partition between the smokers and the non-smokers—the dying and the dead.

A tap on the shoulder. Anna, my always smiling mentor, a leggy blonde originally from Århus. As an undergrad from abroad, I was assigned a Danish graduate student to help me adjust to the country. When I landed in Copenhagen eight months ago, Anna had picked me up from the airport, put me on a bus, and rode her bike beside the 26 until we were in Vesterbro, where her apartment was, where I disembarked and was treated to a home-cooked linguini with ham and cream sauce. I slept on Anna's couch and the next morning, because her tiny place didn't have its own shower, she led me to the public swimming pool where I unsullied myself in the men's locker room. From there, she escorted me to the apartment the university provided me: a converted attic at the top of a treacherous staircase in the home of a brawny and fit eighty-year-old woman. Anna's hospitality was all it took for me to fall a bit in love with her, despite my chances being nil. She was unattached as far as I knew, but two heads taller than me like everyone else in this relentlessly tall and white land.

"Are you coming next week?" Anna asked, referring to a party at her friend's place in Frederiksburg.

"*Ja, selvfølgelig!*" I exclaimed, high-fiving her like an amusement park mascot before she walked away. The sturdy clomping of Anna's winter boots made me envision workmanlike fucking. I was still smiling when my attentions returned to Caroline.

"She's my mentor," I said, sipping the dregs of my espresso. "Her friend's having a party. You should come."

I told her the location, the date, the time. "It'll do you some good," I said. "You should call a hotline or something about what you just told me. I don't know if they have those here. But they should. And you should. We all should."

The more I spoke, the dumber I sounded.

Caroline's expression changed. Disappointment? Relief? I couldn't tell.

I said I had to go to my next class, even though it wasn't for another hour, and scurried off, didn't look back. I fumbled for the near-empty handle of whiskey in my schoolbag and tried to keep my mind on all that mattered to me: making it through another day.

"Whoa," Patrick said when I told him about Caroline. "Has she ever tried?"

"I hope not."

"Maybe she wants you," he said. "A fuck before she jumps."

"Jesus Christ, dude." I went to the bar for another beer. Double-up night at The Moose.

Patrick was one of the new American exchange students. The ones I'd arrived with in the summer had gone home in December, fleeing before the blunt hand of the Scandinavian winter wheeled around. I hardly knew anything about Patrick outside of the fact that he was also from California—Santa Barbara. He was a short white guy, still taller than me by half a head, though some of that height might have been accounted for by his high, shaggy hair.

After drinks that numbered in the double digits, my mind resembled the dimly lit, graffitied, and scribbled-upon walls of The Moose. When Patrick started chatting up a cute Lithuanian girl who could barely speak English, I headed home on the S-Toget. The only other person on the train was a sad-looking woman in her thirties wearing black stretch pants and a mink overcoat. She smoked and swilled from a clear Sprite bottle that was filled with a dark liquid. Her face was red and rubbery. Mine could one day look like hers.

The Svanemøllen stop slid across the window. I got out and considered buying another cheap bottle of red at the kiosk on the way home. Instead, I followed the woman off the train, up the escalator, and out onto the streets. Before she went back to the States, Sylvia, the girl I was in (unrequited) love with last semester, had said, "I can't imagine caring for anyone but myself right now, as ugly as that sounds." We were smoking hash in her room, and she was preempting my confession of feelings for her, the confession I had failed to deliver many times.

"Ugly," I said aloud to no one. The woman glanced over her

shoulder and quickened her step, and soon she was small and distant. I tried to follow the line between sidewalk slabs. The street glistened with fresh rain. I nearly walked into a sign-post. I somehow got back to my apartment. Free from myself, I fell into a poisoned sleep.

Caroline was right. I did understand her. I had tried to kill myself freshman year at Berkeley. My girlfriend Eve, to whom I'd lost my virginity, dumped me because I refused to join the student-led Asian Christian ministry she was in. My parents were calling me every other day to convince me to declare my major in engineering instead of English. During winter break, after all my dormmates left for home, I found myself unable to leave my room. I spent an entire day with my head on my desk, listening to The Smiths' "Please, Please, Please Let Me Get What I Want" on repeat and remembering the softness of Eve's lips against mine and her sleepy-eyed look while we made love. I could've taken BART home, gone back to my old room in my parents' house. But I dreaded seeing them and their hopeful faces, their optimism that I was growing up to become just like them—suburban, Mercedes-driving, company people. I could not imagine doing anything other than what I did; every other possible act—from going for pancakes to taking a piss—seemed overwhelming, like walking in concrete boots.

I popped a bunch of sleeping pills and drank a fifth of whiskey. Had my roommate not come back to get his forgotten acoustic guitar, he wouldn't have found me lying in my puke, and I'd be dead. My parents no longer pressured me about anything. When I revealed I wanted to study abroad the summer after my sophomore year, they were concerned that it was too soon and that I wasn't "healthy" enough. But they agreed after I lied to them, saying that University of Copenhagen had one of the best engineering programs in the world.

"Whatever makes you happy," my dad said. "Make sure that you are happy. Remember to be happy. Please, please remember."

I don't think he'd be happy about my level of achievement in that particular area.

"The question is: 'Can authenticity be represented by metaphor and metonymy?'" Professor Lebowitz said. "And is that representation ironic since metaphor and metonymy are by definition comparative and inauthentic tools?" He chuckled to himself in an otherwise silent classroom.

I slid a note to Patrick, who was sitting to my right. "Every professor here is balding." He muffled a laugh as Professor Lebowitz ran his fingers through his thinning hair and scratched his face, which was pockmarked enough to resemble a Dr. Scholl's pad. Patrick wrote back: "Perhaps you have to donate hair to become a professor here."

During the break, Patrick and I went outside for a smoke under an awning. Three-thirty in the afternoon and the sky was almost black. I struggled to light my cigarette with thick gloves on. Professor Lebowitz joined us and lit all our cigarettes.

"I apologize for this bore of a lecture," he said.

"I wasn't bored," Patrick said. "I still don't understand the whole authenticity-representation relationship, though."

"Authenticity by nature cannot be represented," he said. "The act of representing authenticity is a fraud."

That, I understood. I didn't want to explain to anyone why I had wanted to die, not even to myself. I feared that if I named my feelings, the names would have no authenticity. Part of me wanted to preserve the mystery. Part of me was ashamed. Even while I was in the hospital, I didn't explain myself to my parents. They kept asking, "Why?" like the word was a truncheon. I wanted to feel the pain of disappointing them as punishment. I wanted them to feel pain as well. Professor Lebowitz, who had begun describing metaphor and metonymy again, stopped mid-sentence and cantered after one of his cuter, fresh-faced female students.

"Hey," someone said.

Caroline. She was wearing a Christmas sweater even though it was February, embroidered with a green reindeer and a red-vested snowman.

"What are you doing tonight?" she asked.

I could feel Patrick smirking at me. "I don't know." I turned to him. "What are we doing tonight?"

"I'm going to a poli-sci dinner," he said brightly. "I need to talk to my professor about my paper." He stamped out his cigarette before going back into the classroom. The fucker.

"I'm going to ride the train," Caroline said.

"Where to?"

"Nowhere in particular."

Slush fell on my hand. Then my forehead. Bare tree branches nearby shivered in the wind.

"You live in Østerbro, right?" she said.

"How did you know?"

"Your address was on the student list at the administration."

I imagined Caroline perched on the edge of my bed. Disturbing.

"All right, everyone back in!" Professor Lebowitz called out.

Caroline and I walked through the entrance of Central Station, which had always reminded me of an animal carcass with its giant arches stretching over us like ribs. The spheres of light over the stores made me think of hospital hallways.

"You do this often?" I asked Caroline.

"Every couple of days," she said. "I enjoy the anonymity."

I told her I wanted to stop at one of the convenience stores to get a bottle of red. She followed, apparently not in a hurry. While I stood in line at the checkout counter struggling to read the *Politiken* front pager about President Clinton's upcoming visit, Caroline perused the magazine shelves. I paid for the wine and walked over, figuring she'd be looking at one of the many tabloids featuring Leonardo DiCaprio's dreamy, blue-eyed smile. Instead, she was looking at a porno. I pretended not to notice. She calmly replaced it as if she was setting down a *Der Spiegel*.

On the train, Caroline looked strangely content. Her dark eyes were glossy and reflective. She craned her neck to get a better look at something outside. What was she searching for in all that rain and snow and darkness? I would definitely give Patrick shit about ditching me the next time I saw him. Of course, I could have just as easily ditched Caroline and gone home. That's how badly I wanted company. With the corkscrew on my keychain, I began to open my wine. The conductor announced the Nordhavn stop.

Caroline took me by the arm. "Let's get out."

She dragged me onto the platform, bottle in hand, one station earlier than my stop. The horizon was invisible. The slush has stopped, but the bitter wind made it hard to look at anything too long. The cork finally came loose, though the bottom half remained wedged in the bottle.

"Fuck." I tried to poke the rest of the cork into the wine.

"We're here," she said.

"Where?"

"The first place I wanted to commit suicide in Copenhagen."

The rest of the cork fell into the bottle, squirting wine all over my winter coat. "Fuck-fuck," I said, trying to wipe the stain away. Caroline looked like she was exchanging a smile with a friend standing across the tracks. In the harbor, several cargo ships loomed. Just below the platform lay a row of billboards tagged with graffiti.

"Why here?" I asked.

"The water, the sky," she said. "It's almost as if you can lift the scenery and keep it for yourself."

This girl made me seem like a happy person.

"Why all the drama?" I said, sipping wine grainy with bits of cork. "You're young. We're young. We keep moving, don't we?"

"To your next bottle?"

"Don't underestimate the power of thirty kroner wine from Netto."

The C-Toget interrupted our view. I had a good buzz going already and I was beginning to feel talkative. I even considered telling Caroline about my suicide attempt. Maybe we could compare notes! But when the train going back toward the university arrived, she said, "I'm done with you" and boarded. The bell sounded, the door shut, and just like that, she was gone.

Alone again, I drank more to forget the questions I could not answer, lost where I was and lost where I wanted to go.

"I wish I had come in the summer," Patrick shouted in my ear at Studenterhuset, which was yet again blasting "Wannabe" by Spice Girls. "There were probably way more willing hotties, right?"

I drank my Carlsberg and tried to recall Sylvia's face. She had been gone for only two months, and I was struggling to conjure her already. She had brown hair down to the small of her back and green eyes. The Sylvia I remembered looked like that of a pale, doe-eyed anime character.

It was a Monday and the place was nearly empty. After the first few weeks of feverish mixer activities, students were starting to stay home and study, or perhaps they were like me: uninterested in the people they'd met.

"At least you're exotic and adorable here," Patrick said. "Like a toy or a pet."

I let the first few similes go, but he continued, thinking he was funny. He had been saying that he wanted to become a standup comedian, though he'd never been on stage for any reason. When he said I was like a bullet vibrator, I finished the rest of my beer and said I was going home.

"But we're not even buzzed yet," Patrick said.

"You're a complete waste, you know that?" I said. "I can see your time here will be lost on you."

Patrick backed away, looking wounded. "I was just joking, man."

Like my broken-corked wine, there was no recorking my outburst. I got on my bike and wobbled to Christiania, where I bought a small brick of hash, sat at a table alone in one of the cafes, and quietly, slowly rolled and consumed one joint after another. My time here had been such a waste. There, in the haze and the stench of cannabis smoke, dreadlocks, and wet dogs, I tried to recall Sylvia's face again, but it was Caroline's that came to me. A smiling, grown-up version of her. A version that liked herself. A version that people wanted to be around. Wasn't that the definition of attractiveness?

This party was way out in Frederiksberg and there was a forecasted sleet storm. I considered staying in, doubting that people would travel that far out in this weather, even for the *hyggelig*: the Danish concept of hospitality—good food, friends, and candlelight. But in the end, I decided to go. I walked several long blocks in the freeze from the S-Toget stop to the apartment complex.

When I arrived, the living room was already jammed with Danes holding clear plastic cups tinted pink with drink. Patrick had his arm around some blonde girl. I had no idea what girls found interesting about him, but he seemed to find it easy to hook up. Probably because average-looking white guys had a better chance with the ladies than the best-looking Asian guy. When I asked him where the drinks were, he wordlessly pointed to the kitchen, the only room lit by electricity and not candles. I scanned for Anna or someone I could appear to know, but there was nobody. I squeezed through the forest of tall Danes to the kitchen where, of all people, Professor Lebowitz held court, red-faced and laughing with a pair of brunettes.

"Boy, you look like the weather has gotten the best of you," he said to me.

My teeth were still chattering, but the apartment was so artificially warm that I was damp with sweat.

"Where's your cup?" Professor Lebowitz raised a tall bottle of Schnapps.

"I was just going to get one."

He pointed up. "Top floor."

I went down a hallway, out a door, and suddenly I was in a cold stairwell. I walked up three flights of stairs and into a large, dimly lit dining hall or ballroom that felt like the meeting place of a secret society. To the left was a round table surrounded by plush recliners. To the right was a bar, and directly in front of me was a hallway leading to more rooms. I searched for plastic cups. Sure enough, they lay next to a red till, which was open and unlocked with hundreds of kroners inside.

We were supposed to pitch in for the booze. Danish honor system.

Under the bar, I discovered several full cases of beer. An icebox behind me was also full of Carlsberg and Tuborg, and since there was no one pining for me downstairs, I decided to knock down a few to get myself social before heading back. I sat at the table with three open Carlsbergs, relishing the silence.

"Hey," someone said.

Startled, I nearly spit up my beer.

Caroline again. She sat across from me. Too much makeup.

Looked like she'd tried unsuccessfully to curl her hair. She was wearing a puce-colored dress that was too big on her.

"What are you doing up here?" I said.

"These things are not usually fun for me."

"It'll be fun after a couple of these," I said, tipping my beer back.

"Did you come because you like your mentor?"

I blushed. "Oh please," I said. "I hardly know her."

"But the way you look at her."

"Men tend to look at women that way."

"Not all women."

"Of course not all," I said, averting her gaze.

I slid one of my beers across the table.

"What do you see in drinking?" she asked, eyeing the bottle with disgust.

"I guess I need to feel guilty about something," I said. "It's what I'm best at."

Caroline remained quiet.

"This is where you're supposed to say, 'That's a horrible thing to say about yourself,'" I said.

"You're not horrible," she said. "Just ugly."

The words hit me in the face like the S-Toget. I started feeling like I did that day in the dorms, not long after Eve told me that if she had to choose between loving Christ and loving me, the choice couldn't be more obvious. Caroline said she was going downstairs, but I hardly heard her. I just sat there, her words echoing in my ears. After I finished the Carlsbergs, I went for more. People started trickling into the room. My head was reeling. I couldn't remember how many drinks I'd had. Suddenly, Anna was sitting on the arm of my chair. I felt nauseous, the smell of smoke gripping my lungs. I tried to smile; she looked like an Aphrodite in winter in a black turtleneck dress, leggings, and knee-high boots. My head rested against her right hip as she laughed with some blond guy wearing rimless glasses. She stroked my head, and for a moment the nausea went away.

"He's drunk again," she said to her friend. "Just like last week. And the week before that. I hope he doesn't vomit. He's a nice guy. With *store problemer*."

They laughed. Any response from me would have been accompanied by my breakfast, lunch, and dinner. Anna left me for the window.

"It's snowing," she said.

"Let's go see," her friend suggested. They left. I stood slowly, hoping a little fresh air might make me feel whole again.

I eventually found my way out of the building. Snowflakes fell lightly on my skin, and a blast of cold air made me shudder. A full layer had frosted the cars, and the ground was packed white. Anna and her friend threw snowballs at each other in the street. I fell to my knees and puked. I tried to puke Caroline's words. I tried to puke my parents' expectations. I tried to puke my unrequited loves. I tried to puke the embarrassment of being me: a short, thin, ugly, unlovable young Asian man. Tears came to eyes as I retched again and again. I lay on my back, the snow hitting my face. I imagined being run over and what a relief that would be.

Desperately wanting to sleep, I heard slushy footsteps. Anna and her friend hovered over me.

I had interrupted them, I thought as I passed out.

I woke the next afternoon, missing all my classes. I had no recollection of how I got back to my apartment. My landlady had slipped an envelope beneath the door. It contained a letter on resume paper with loopy, florid handwriting from a fountain pen:

By the time you read this, I'll be gone. There's little use of being noble about something like this. I quit because I can't cope with being bigger and better on the inside than I am on the outside. I can't stand being invisible anymore. I'm not curious about the rest of my life.

I came to Copenhagen hoping to find the courage to live. Instead, I found the courage to admit defeat. I've accepted that the land of love is closed to some. I am ignored and condescended to everywhere, like a pet. There are the beautiful and the ugly. I wish that the world didn't force others to lie to me about which group I'm in.

Let me tell you a little bit about myself:

I love my Mom but I'll always remember that she didn't like the way I looked. She pushed me to dermatologists and makeover specialists from the time I was ten or eleven. She never loved my Dad, but she never diminished him in my eyes. For that, I give her credit. My Dad is a quiet and supportive man. The night before I came to Copenhagen, he said he hoped I would find what I was looking for.

He's the only person who ever understood that there was something missing for me. It hurts me to know that my choice will hurt him.

I had a best friend named Diane. We were at this bar two years ago in Seattle. An ever-so-pretentious guy started talking to us. Tall Timothy with that goatee he never touched for some reason. I thought he sat down next to us to talk to me. But it was Diane he wanted. She went home with him. That night I cried, replaying my conversation with him over and over, until that distant, distracted look Timothy used to hold me off branded itself in my memory. Diane liked to say I was beautiful. I never believed her, and I knew she didn't believe it herself. I was her friend so that she could feel more beautiful.

You're the only person I was curious about in Copenhagen. You gave me that look Timothy gave me. Last night, I just couldn't take it anymore. At a certain point of loneliness, every person is just another who won't love you, another who can't get beyond himself. Everyone knows you're drinking yourself to death. You hate yourself for everything you do and everything you don't.

You're the last person I had a crush on.

Love,
Caroline

I tried to read the note once more but couldn't. It was too raw, too similar to how I felt, like she was writing out her insides and mine. Had she really gone through with it? Did I give her the final push onto the tracks?

I thumbed through a newspaper to see if anyone had been hit by a train. I went to the exchange program office and asked for Caroline's address. They said she had dropped out at the beginning of the week.

She'd told the administration that she had to fly home for a family emergency. I asked for her American contact info, saying I had something of hers I needed to return. I called her mother.

"She's in Copenhagen," she said. "Want me to give you her number?"

When I went to her apartment in Nørrebro, the landlord, one of the few short, dark-haired Danish men I'd seen, said she had moved out just yesterday.

As the mid-afternoon darkness descended, I started to believe she had indeed done what she said she would.

The train to Østerbro was crowded. I was forced to squeeze against the windows in the smoke-filled cabins because the guy next to me was obese. A leathery middle-aged woman stumbled into the car and sat across from me muttering in Danish. The woman stank of bourbon and wore floral tights and a tatty fur coat.

"*Min maend siger, jeg er grim,*" she said loudly. "*Min maend siger, jeg er skidtgrim.*"

"*Nej, det er du ikke,*" I said, and I was telling the truth. She was not ugly. Her man was abusive.

"*Nordhavn Sta-cion*," the speaker said. The train came slowly to a stop, the whistle sounded, and the doors parted. I looked out the window, and there she was, staring right at me:

Caroline. I hurried onto the platform.

She smirked, wearing a too-large wool sweater.

"I just mailed a note to my parents," she said. "In a few days, they'll think I'm dead."

"Where did you sleep?"

She said she'd checked into a hotel.

We stood in silence. I searched for words. She started sobbing. I put an arm around her. A powerful gust funneled through the platform, and I shuddered, my breath smoking in the air.

"I've never been that close before," she said. "Train after train went by."

Snow began to fall. We sat, rocking slowly to keep warm. She gathered her backpack and got up as the next train to Høje Taastrup arrived. I didn't want her to leave. Tomorrow, she'd be back again, repeating her sad ritual until one day, the trains would be late.

"So you're going to drink again tonight, I guess," she said, rubbing her nose.

The reproach in her words stopped me from replying. I had my own sad ritual. As the train grinded to a halt, I said, "I won't drink if you won't jump."

Caroline looked at me. I couldn't tell what she was thinking.

"Do you really think I'm ugly?" I asked as the train's whistle sounded.

"What?" she asked.

I grabbed her hand. "Don't go. Please."

The doors closed, and the B-Toget sped off, bending in the distance. The ocean shimmered from last daylight, and we continued to wait for a train to take us to a home we didn't know.

"I tried once," I said. I'd never heard myself say the words aloud. My confession made me feel real, flesh and blood, like an authentic person. "I was heartbroken and my feelings avalanched and I couldn't control them. I was scared by how far I went. I'm still scared now."

"I'm scared, too," Caroline said.

When the next train came, we stepped forward, toeing the yellow line. I didn't know where she was going, but I was not leaving her.

Inside, we took a seat by the window, and I watched the sea, the water blank behind the falling snow, the smokestacks, and the flitting bare trees. I ignored the cigarette smoke, the alcoholics, the immobile elderly, and the obnoxious children. There was just the sea the color of a wolf's coat, as if the train rode on the surface of the water, as if we could just pick up the scenery and keep it with us forever.

Caroline rested her head on my shoulder, and when she shut her eyes, I looked at her face and felt, for the first time, found.

8

League of Losers

Gents,

It's been a long winter in more ways than one, and I know I haven't spoken to many of you since the end of last season when I hoisted the League of Losers pennant for a record-breaking 4th time in our fifteen-year history. I hope all of you have sufficiently licked your wounds, and I hope you and your families are doing well.

The last several months have been a roller coaster of emotions for me, and I wanted to share my experience with my Chi brothers.

On December 9, my first son, Johnson Wong III, was born healthy and strong. Thirteen weeks later, he continues to bring unspeakable joy to me and my wife Maryanna.

On December 19, one day before my 38th birthday, my younger brother Barry passed away unexpectedly in his home. Two days prior to his death, Barry had a diagnostic colonoscopy performed to confirm a Crohn's diagnosis. He was sent home following the procedure and went to work the next day. An autopsy revealed a perforation in his bowels that led to a fatal infection.

Barry was my idol. A few of you have had the privilege of meeting and spending time with him. He was an accomplished musician, painter, and filmmaker. Yesterday, I attended what would have been his 34th birthday party. When I saw his enlarged picture on a foam board, I thought this could not be happening to me. Had my wife and kids not been there, I would not have made it through the day. I miss Barry with an intensity I never knew possible. Millions time worse than back in 2003, when I lost the League of Losers championship on the final day thanks to my horrific decision to spot-start Jose Lima versus Esteban Loaiza. Only 18 months ago, I was the best man at Barry's wedding. All the clichés are true and then some. Life can change in an instant. Cherish each moment you have. Don't take any day for granted.

Barry is survived by his wife Michelle and their 3 children (Marjorie, age 6; Timothy, age 3; Kristi, age 2). Please consider making a contribution to the Barry Wong Family Memorial Fund (link in PDF attached). It would mean a lot to me.

Your friend and defending champion,

JW2

Johnson Wong II
Director, Partner Relationship Development
Google

———

Guys—holy shit. How do we respond?

El Hays

———

Tried to make a donation, but the link is broken.

Gordon Rodriguez
Vice President, Global Accounts
JP Morgan Chase

———

Should we send him a note of condolence?

Theodore

———

Managers—I think our donation/condolences/response should come from the league as a whole. What do you guys think? I can draft a response and run it by everyone. Perhaps we can dedicate this year's winnings to Barry Wong's family?

The Commish

———

I don't know about the rest of the managers, but there's NO way I'd support donating this year's prize pot. In fifteen years, we've NEVER discussed donating the pot to anyone other than the winning manager for ANY reason. The Schmitt Schlitt's Mitts has finished no lower than 3rd in the past three years, and our roster of keepers has never been stronger. My staff of Clayton Kershaw, Madison Bumgarner, and Yu Darvish, ALL on discount deals, make me a clear favorite this year. I'd understand that for other managers, donating the pot seems like the honorable thing to do, but I guarantee you those managers aren't favorites for the title this season. Honestly, I don't even think we should put this dumb idea to a vote.

No offense, Commish.

Bob

Schmitt Schlitt's Mitts

———

Jesus, JW2, my thoughts are with you.

You are still playing this year, right?

Chang

———

Thanks, Chang. I was wondering where everyone went.

Of course I'll be playing. I need to do some normal things to get my mind off what has happened. I think Barry would want it that way. He was never into sports much, and sometimes I feel like maybe I paid too much attention to sports when I could've devoted more time to connecting with him.

If I'm you guys, I see an opening to the title this year. I don't know if I can give my franchise the attention it needs.

Good to hear from you!

JW2

———

JW2—congrats on the new baby. Now that you have a kid, I hope you'll be unable to concentrate on managing your team. HAHA!

I'm interested in a pre-draft trade for Max Scherzer. I've put together a SWEETHEART deal for you. Go into ESPN and check it out!

Let me know!

Bob

Schmitt Schlitt's Mitts

———

You gotta be fucking kidding me, right? Five guys you're going to cut anyway for an AL Cy Young Winner?

JW2

———

J—We're sincerely sorry for the loss of your brother. We've decided as a group to donate $20 to Brian's family through the link you sent. The League of Losers' prayers are with you at this time.

On a personal note, I got a chance to meet your brother that weekend in Vegas at your bachelor's party. Even though I didn't get any of the cultural references he kept making, I found him to be an incredibly nice guy. I still remember the lap dance he got for both you and me at Cheetah's. Wow, remember Nikki Day? I still see that girl in my dreams (and sometimes on the Internet). Anyway, hard to believe that Brian's gone. Very eerie when someone so clear in your memories doesn't actually exist anymore.

Separately, I've donated another $5 in my name.

Good fucking luck this season. We're all dedicating this year to Brian. I've changed the name of the league on ESPN to League of Losers: Brian's Song.

Best,
Commish

Arnold Tell
Managing Director, Derivatives Trading
UBS

———

HOLY FUCK, Arn, JW's brother is named BARRY, not Brian. I thought you were going to run a draft of the message by us!

Bob

Schmitt Schlitt's Mitts

———

Omg I'm an idiot

Commish

Sent from my iPhone

———

Attention to detail is why Big Motherfucking Rally Mongers are always near the bottom of the league.

Gordon Rodriguez
Vice President, Global Accounts
JP Morgan Chase

———

I'm glad we were able to send Barry's future generations to school with our $20 donation.

Theodore

———

Fk, I'll draft a new one and run it by everyone. I work at UBS. We're used to damage control.

Commish

———

LELAND CHEUK

Commish—Forget it, man. I'll send something and blind copy you guys. I'm the only one here who has any humanity left.

Best,
Chang

———

JW—I'm sincerely sorry about Arn's email. That guy is seriously autistic. That or a sociopath. Maybe both. I'm also sorry about how long it's taken for me to reach out to you personally. My favorite memory of Barry was day 2 of your bachelor's party when I said I didn't like to gamble, and Arn and the others were making fun of me like no tomorrow about how I was a shitty Asian and all that. Barry never partook. I think I was tired of the ribbing by like the first hour of the first day. He and I were standing in line for the bathroom at Hooters and he said quietly, out of nowhere: "I hate gambling, too. I don't know why an Asian not gambling is so funny to everyone." That's the type of guy Barry was, right? No bullshit. You know better than I.

Please let me know if I can do anything to help during this time of grieving. I'd fly out to New York in a second. You know I'm here for you. At least, I hope you still know after that fucking travesty of an email by Arn. I have two brothers; the three of us are also very close. Don't know what I'd do without them. Can't imagine the pain you're going through.

Your bud,
Chang

————

Hey man –

I really appreciate your note. Thanks for thinking of me. For the past three weeks, I've been wondering whether to continue on with the League of Losers. I guess on top of losing my brother, I've begun to wonder whether we're all actually friends. I didn't receive one phone call, not one text. A bunch of you stood with me at my wedding as groomsmen. I guess that's what it means to grow older. You have your own jobs in your own cities with your own families, and our friendship just becomes something that happened a long time ago, when we were different people.

I know I tend to be really effusive and passionate about our fantasy league, and you guys probably think I'm that passionate about the rest of my life, but I'm not. I'm just a cowardly corporate whore who reserves his risky moves for a game we play on a computer. My brother put his heart out there every day of his life. In every piece of work he did, every relationship he built. He didn't have Plan B's like the rest of us. He ended up sacrificing a steady living to do what he loved. Ultimately, he sacrificed his life because he could only afford care from a substandard hospital.

But guys like us? Guys like the League of Losers? Nothing bad ever happens to us.

I'm really glad you got to know him, even if it was just for a short time.

Still bros,
JW2

Johnson Wong II
Director, Partner Relationship Development
Google

———

Gents,

Thanks for doing what you can. Look forward to kicking all your fucking asses during the draft this weekend.

The Defending Champ,

Johnson Wong II
Manager and Owner—The Wongtowers

9

Funeral By The Arcade

Eddie Wu and I weren't close. I was just his English tutor. When his granddaughter informed me he'd been killed by a hit-and-run driver, I was sad and shocked, of course, but in an unsettled and detached manner—like one might react to news of the passing of a distant friend on Facebook. To my surprise, I was invited to the funeral in Monterey Park, where Eddie lived, my hometown.

On the morning of, I froze at the sight of my black suit hanging from a towel rod like a headless torso. My air passages narrowed. Anxiety's precipice.

I didn't want to go.

The population of Monterey Park was nearly two-thirds Chinese. More storefront signs were in hanzi characters than in English. One year, during the Chinese New Year's Day parade, the city put up banners that misspelled the town name (Montrey Park). My parents didn't have a single non-Chinese friend or acquaintance and couldn't read or write English. I was over that world. The insularity. The expectations. The guilt.

It took me two hours to get there from Manhattan Beach thanks to rush-hour traffic. During the drive, I tried not to think about how close the funeral home was to the house I grew up in, where my mother still lived. Just a ten-minute walk away, a ninety-second drive.

At the funeral home the lot was full, so I parked around the corner from my mother's house and walked over, holding a large bouquet of flowers. A van pulled into the lot. When the driver got out and began unloading funeral wreaths on easels, I realized that bringing flowers like I was going on a first date was a mistake—not a custom in a traditional Buddhist funeral. I returned the bouquet to my car, checked my reflection in the window of the back seat. I looked strange. My spiked hair was especially coarse and unkempt, and my skin tone resembled that of someone who'd just stepped out of a tanning salon. I hadn't worn my suit in years, and it was too big for me now; I looked like a kid wearing his father's clothes.

Near the entrance, a shrunken, silver-haired woman wearing a black embroidered vest was surrounded by a cluster of high-school-aged girls, one of whom I recognized as Eddie's granddaughter. Eddie's wife and the rest of his grandchildren, I presumed. I introduced myself to Mrs. Wu as Eddie's English tutor and offered my condolences in broken Cantonese. Eddie's granddaughter, who dropped Eddie off at my place for his lessons, shook my hand and thanked me for coming. I blanked on her name, so I just said, "You're welcome" and smiled dumbly. She waved me through the entrance, emanating pity or amusement—I couldn't decide which.

The interior was deep and wide but low-ceilinged, the size and feel of a hotel ballroom rented for small trade shows. A long table stretched across the center of the room and featured a red-and-gold papier-mâché shrine that displayed a photograph of Eddie in an ornate frame, cardboard staging props of a toy racecar, and a flat screen television. Nice cars and TVs. Things Eddie liked. In the photo, he looked bewildered, trapped. There were several rows of chairs on either side of the shrine, stretching toward the entrance. Against the back wall, the wreaths stood next to a brick fireplace.

In front of Eddie's photo, there was a sand-filled urn pierced with numerous burnt incense sticks. The man in front of me drew a fresh one, fired it up, squeezed it in his palms, bowed several times, and inserted it in the sand. I followed suit. Lighting the red end, I speared my stick into the urn with authority. Even my father might have been proud of the force with which I speared said stick. Then I noticed my offering looked different from the others. The red end was supposed to be in the sand. I had never lit incense before and had fired up the wrong end. Embarrassed, I spun and bumped into a man who said something in Mandarin, which of course I didn't understand. I pretended not to hear him and milled about, not knowing what to do next. No one was sitting. People were wandering just like me, like we were in an art gallery. In a far corner of the room, there was a red tent inside of which four monks were getting dressed—buttoning red robes, putting on round, black hats. About a dozen mourners stood outside, scattered in groups of three or four. They appeared solemn, but no one was crying or even teary-eyed.

Was this what my father's funeral was like? Did many attend? Probably. He was popular in the community. An acupuncturist, he was known as King Needle. His face graced a billboard on Garvey Boulevard. People must have cried for the King.

After I got all As in seventh grade, I talked my dad into buying me a computer game of my choosing. *Quake* was the gift he would come to regret giving. The moment I set unseen feet upon the pixilated corridors of that dungeonesque military base, I was teleported—slipgated, if you will. *Quake* became my daydream machine. The discipline I'd previously poured into schoolwork went into these death matches. I began an Olympian's training regimen. I played eight hours a day, every day. I cut classes to work at a place named The Arcade, where, in exchange for my sitting behind the counter while Walt the owner went surfing, I got to practice on the PCs and consoles. I became so good that when I'd play kids in my neighborhood, they'd rarely inflict damage on me. The Arcade was about a half-mile from where I was now.

I began competing in tournaments and winning. A thousand dollars here. Five grand there. I got my first corporate sponsor after winning a tourney in Santa Monica. My parents knew about my growing gaming powers, but they didn't understand why companies sent me these big checks to deposit into my college fund. They thought I was involved in some form of illegal gambling. I tried to explain the world of competitive gaming numerous times, but after thousands of puzzled looks, I stopped trying.

I was just seventeen when I won an all-expenses-paid spot at the World Series of Gaming in Amsterdam. My handle was DiggNiddy; it was what I let my opponents die with. Had my monitor not gone on the fritz for a split-second versus The Slovak, I would've been champ. I never told my mother I was going to Europe. She thought I was at some science camp. She called the mothers of my friends and discovered I was overseas, and there was no way to reach me. I didn't have an international cell phone plan. My mother didn't use email. I had no idea that while I was killing opponent after opponent on a screen, a heart attack had killed my father.

I got home two days after he had been buried. I rang the doorbell with my ridiculous silver trophy inside the duffel slung over my shoulder, and my mother opened the door and screamed that I was not her son, that no son of hers could be so heartless, that no good son would have left her to bury my father alone. She said she didn't want to see my selfish face again. Then she inadvertently called me by my father's Chinese name. She slammed the door in my face, didn't answer my calls in the subsequent days, weeks, and months.

That was ten years ago.

Outside, steam rose from an open tent at the other end of the parking lot. The smell of wok grease sweetened the morning air. A round, broad-shouldered, and tall young man—an XL-sized kid, really—appeared at my side.

"If you want something to eat," he said, motioning toward the tent, "feel free."

I told him no thanks, even though I was hungry. I had forgotten to eat breakfast.

"How did you know Grandpa?" he said.

This kid was twice Eddie's size. When I told him I was Eddie's English tutor, his eyes widened and his mouth gaped. "He told me about you!" he exclaimed. "You're the video game king! You're DiggNiddy!"

"I was never king," I said. "I finished second once."

"Second in the world, man!"

"That was a long time ago."

"Do you still play?"

135

I had been retired for five years. I had bought a place with the money I made from my branded computer mice, mouse pads, and laptop cases. "It's a younger man's game," I said. "You'd be the perfect age. Do you play?"

"Fuck yeah, I play."

"You good?"

"I'm not bad," he said. "I play online." He clapped me on the back, grinning down upon me like a Laughing Buddha. "Damn, I'd love to play video games professionally."

"Do you know The Arcade?" I pointed west, in its general direction. "That's where I practiced."

"So, are you, like, rich now?"

Chinese people are blunt, I was reminded. "I'm lucky," I said.

He introduced himself as Calvin.

I said I was sorry for his loss, and his eyes clouded. "It was an accident," he said, kicking a gravel pebble onward. "There was no way he could have avoided it." The quiet way he said those words twisted something tender inside, made me think of the suddenness of my father's death and how one's game could end at any second. In video games, the fear of the sudden propels you forward. Not so in life.

Calvin leaned toward the food tent. "I need to eat."

My stomach growled more insistently, so I followed him.

We ordered bowls of congee and fried dough sticks. I missed Chinese food. When my father worked late, instead of cooking in, my mother would buy roast pork, heat it up, and sauté some Chinese broccoli with oyster sauce and garlic. That would be my death row meal. I gave up Chinese food for gaming. Too much gluten. I feared mental lassitude. You need a responsive, active body to be the foundation for what your eyes see and what the mind interprets.

Calvin said he was a senior in high school planning to go to Pasadena City College. His parents wanted him to be an investment banker. I nodded, pretending to be thoughtful, even though I didn't know anything about investment banking, community college, or the alleged existence of an overlap of the two worlds. I never went to college, because I went into the pro-gaming circuit. Calvin asked where I lived, and when I answered Manhattan Beach, he looked at me like I'd said Kyrgyzstan.

"It's a great place to live," I said. "I run on the beach every morning. It can't get much better."

"Isn't West L.A. like super-white?"

"There are people like us there."

"Wow," Calvin said, shaking his head, slurping the remains of his congee. He motioned one of the servers for another bowl. I hadn't finished half of mine.

Calvin out-ate me five bowls to two. By the time we returned to the funeral home, a crowd was slowly entering. Many of the seats inside were now occupied. The funeral was finally about to begin. Being around this many Chinese people again made me jittery. I felt all eyes were on me, like it was only a matter of time before I'd be put in front of the room, inspected for my muscle definition and dental health, and sold to a pair of authoritative parents seeking a child to spirit off to medical school.

One other person appeared as out-of-place as I felt: a dark-haired white man in his thirties. He was checking his phone, saving the open seat beside him with a messenger bag. As I looked for an unoccupied chair, the man cleared the seat without looking up.

I thanked him as I sat. "How do you know Eddie?"

He had a stubbly, sharp chin and a nose that was Z-lined from being broken and improperly set. "I'm a friend of his grandson."

"Him?" I pointed to Calvin, whose back was turned to me as he greeted one of his relatives.

"No." The man returned his attentions to his machine.

One monk unfurled a sizable rug in front of Eddie's shrine. To the women in the room, a second handed out pointy white cloth caps that resembled mini-Klansmen hoods. Rounded caps, each marked with a red dot, were given to the men. A third monk motioned for several people to remove their shoes and kneel on the rug.

I put on my cap and asked Calvin what was happening. He said the hoods warded off evil spirits but then confessed he really had no clue. In Cantonese, Calvin asked his mother, who was among the kneelers. She didn't reply because another woman tapped her on the shoulder and they hugged each other and began bawling.

"I'll ask her later," Calvin said.

He began to banter idly with Eddie's granddaughters. They poked fun at him for once admitting that Ariana Grande was hot. Calvin issued firm denials. He was a Taylor Swift guy. Ooh, you prefer older ladies, one of the cousins teased. Calvin guffawed, bear-hugging the twig-limbed girl until she almost vanished in his grasp.

Eddie's family seemed to genuinely care about each other. Their filial fettle probably had something to do with Eddie.

Eddie and my dad were born the same year, and they were nothing alike. Eddie embraced just about everything about his new country. He was fearless when it came to chatting up people of all races. He desired English fluency so he could apply for American citizenship. He said he didn't want to be like his son, who owned a chain of Chinese restaurants in the San Gabriel Valley and bragged that he had made his millions without learning a word of English, without ever even voting. He asked his granddaughter to use "Goo-go" to find a tutor who wouldn't speak Cantonese to him. When we first met, he was dressed like a character out of the musical *Grease*. His gray hair was slicked back with goop, and he wore a white short-sleeve dress shirt and a skinny dark tie.

"Chinese," he said in English during our first lesson. "We get so comfort! Even my grandkid don't go out from Mon-trey Pok. We come from so far China, and now we never leave one small village?"

"I left," I said.

Eddie guffawed. "You still in L.A., man!"

He learned to speak English really well but struggled with reading and writing. I made him read tabloids aloud because the written English was roughly third-grade level. He loved repeating the headlines. When his granddaughter picked him up from my place, Eddie would show off.

"Katy Perry and Tay-la Swift talk on phone this week and Katy still very mad!"

His granddaughter giggled. "It's Tay-lor."

"We're working on the names," I said.

We spent one session diagramming sentences. Man, did

he hate that! I knew he'd hate it, too. Anything that involved putting pencil to paper, Eddie despised.

"Object…proposition…werb…who care?" he growled, his hands grasping the air like a blind man trying to catch falling prizes. My father used a similar hand gesture when he was frustrated. Like every time he told me that I'd never make as much money gaming as I would performing acupuncture.

"You want to be an American citizen, don't you?" I said to Eddie. "The test will require that you write."

"Re-kwai?"

"It means 'you have to.' Like my dad used to say, 'You have to do well in school.'"

"I talk very good."

"You speak well. I agree. But there are no shortcuts."

Eddie sighed and laid his pencil on the table. He raised the workbook to his face, his nose nearly grazing the pages. He seemed to be trying to decode something. Then he flattened the book and picked up the pencil. "No short cot," he muttered.

He sounded exactly like my father when I'd tell him gaming was work. King Needle would say: No short cot in life. Work no fun; that's why it work.

The monks chanted in a barely comprehensible dialect. A dense smoke stung my eyes. A gray-haired woman fed pastel-colored funny money one slip at a time into the now-lit fireplace. It was raining outside and all the doors were closed. Thirteen people, Calvin included, were on their knees, squeezed onto the rug. They were Eddie's immediate family: his siblings, children, and grandchildren.

There had been a number of rituals—lots of chanting and bowing—and all of it was lost on me. One of Eddie's sons was inconsolable; he had been sobbing continuously for an hour. At first I felt sympathy, but soon I wanted to hit the mute button. I straightened in my chair, trying not to yawn or roll my eyes. A woman handed out bottled water like we were participating in an athletic event.

When others got up to stretch their legs, I followed. I paced the length of the windows and considered walking over to The Arcade. I imagined The Arcade of my adolescence. The bright blue awning. The white letters. The green neon open sign. A gong sounded. I experienced a sudden yearning to play there again—a reflex, long lost.

A monk announced that Eddie's grandchildren were allowed to break for lunch. Calvin limped stiff-legged to my side, and we headed out into the rain toward the meal tent.

"My mom said that in the old days, back in China, they'd be on their knees for a week," he said. "They'd have to crawl to go to the bathroom."

"How long is this going to last?"

"I think they're serving dinner."

I cussed silently. The white man passed, walking in silence beside an Asian one of roughly the same height. They spoke without looking at each other.

"That's my cousin," Calvin said.

"Yeah?"

"He and that guy are...you know."

"Together?" I said, not entirely surprised. "They've been fighting."

"Nobody wanted them to come," Calvin said. "They're disgusting."

I grew up with many children of immigrants like Calvin,

and there were two camps: those who didn't question traditions and those who did.

"They're happy," I said. "What's the big deal?"

Calvin's eyes hardened. "Maybe that's the way they think where you live."

"Nobody wins trying to keep others from being happy."

"You won!" Calvin exclaimed. "You're the video game king!"

"That's not what I'm saying."

"You're King DiggNiddy!" he said, his smile lambent. He smacked me on the arm and repeated who I used to be.

Inside the tent, steam billowed from large pots and woks. We sat at a ten-top with Calvin's cousin, his partner, and six sexagenarian women I didn't know. Servers brought out plates of ginger chicken, roast pork, and fried catfish. We took off our absurd white hats and ate.

A Kangol-wearing woman asked Calvin's cousin whether he had a girlfriend yet and opined he needed one soon because he was getting old. Calvin's cousin half-smiled and agreed but said he was too busy. His partner typed furiously on his phone. The woman eyed him for a long moment before asking Calvin whether he had a girlfriend.

"I have lots of them," Calvin said in Cantonese.

Laughter around the table.

The woman squinted and pointed at him. "Don't play around. Forget girls. Focus on school."

Then she turned to me. "What's your family name?"

"I don't speak much Chinese," I said in English.

The table quieted and the woman's shoulders sagged.

"Another one of them," she said in Cantonese to the rest of the table.

"He's from Monterey Park," Calvin blurted. "He's a championship video game player."

"Ask him his family name," the woman said.

Calvin forked chicken and ate. "What's your last name?" he asked, mouth full.

I cleared my throat and said my last name in Cantonese.

"Oh, he speaks!" the woman said. "He speaks pretty well. I thought you said you didn't speak."

"Only a few words."

"You're still speaking!" she said. "I know your mother. Have you seen her since you've come home? She says you never come home."

My insides tumbled. For a vertiginous moment, the women all looked like my mother: unusually tall, hunched, eyes wide apart, high and prominent cheekbones. Her hair would be gray now. I sipped tepid tea, felt the pulse in my neck, tried to appear unmoved.

"Jimmy was Eddie's English tutor," Calvin said.

"Your mother misses you," the woman said. "She told me."

A bitter lump rose in my throat. I shrugged dumbly, as if the past decade—being separated from her, from my home-town—meant nothing. My mother gave up on me. She told me never to return. She never sought me out. But these were words I couldn't say in Cantonese to this stranger.

The others asked the woman who my mother was. Some knew her well. She was managing a Chinese restaurant. They agreed that my absence explained a lot. They had always assumed that she was just sad because she was a widow. One woman joked that she wouldn't be sad if her husband died because she'd been looking forward to claiming his half of the bed for decades. The rest of the table laughed, but I couldn't. I tunnel-visioned the food. The catfish was eviscerated, its spine twisted so that the bones pointed skyward, the gaping mouth pleading for help not given. Calvin's cousin's boyfriend stood, wearing a plastic smile.

"You lovely ladies have to eat!" he exclaimed, ladling roast pork onto plates. There was sarcasm in his outsized and sudden display of charm. He and I exchanged glances. He was trying to divert attention from me. He thought, as I did, that the Chinese were being intrusive. Calvin's cousin glared at him, while Calvin held a hand over his plate, refusing to be served.

I pushed back from the table and escaped into open air. The rain had stopped and the sun had emerged. I stood in the parking lot between two cars: one a Mercedes, the other a pickup truck. Both license plates were personalized with the owner's last names (in this case, Lee and Lam) and then 168, numbers that, when spoken in Cantonese, rhyme with the phrase "one road to riches." That was the problem with the Chinese. There was only one road to riches. The road your elders approved of. I slowly got wet. I shouldn't have come to the funeral, I thought. I wanted to keep moving forward. Onto the next level of my game.

With each passing year, my mother had become a tumescent presence inside me. In dreams, I saw her face that day I returned home from Amsterdam: twisting, wringing, the stretching and melting of her hard features. I sometimes tried to remember my mother well—draw a version of her that included good memories. But I mostly remembered the criticisms. She didn't like my haircut, too spiky. She didn't like that I sat around gaming for hours; it made my butt big. She didn't think I drank enough milk or water; that's why I wasn't tall like white people. Like my father, she wasn't an affectionate person. There was one thing she could always be positive about:

My baby pictures. "You were so cute back then," she said once while showing me yellowed photos she planned to frame. Then she looked me up and down. I could see her resisting the urge to physically inspect the high school version of me: my skin, my tongue, my limbs, everything. She turned away, ever disappointed.

Calvin emerged from the tent. "Sorry about my aunt."

"I should have stayed home today."

Calvin smacked me hard on the arm. "Aw, come on! Then you wouldn't have met me." He flashed a wide, whisker-framed grin that made me smile.

"You're lucky to have this," I said, motioning toward the Chinese masses in the tent.

Calvin looked upon me like he was questioning my sanity. "Why don't you ever come home?"

Air passages were narrowing again. Anxiety, a friend, my tutor. "Long story," I said, inhaling the comforting scent of wet asphalt.

"Wanna swing by The Arcade?" I said. "It's not far."

"With DiggNiddy?" Calvin exclaimed. "Hells yeah!"

We walked along the boulevard several long blocks, passing a bubble tea joint, a noodle house with no English name, a restaurant named the Hot Pot Spot, a post office, and an East West Bank. Then there it was, The Arcade. That bright blue

145

awning I had imagined was now faded and tattered. The white "r" and "e" had fallen out of the name, leaving "The A cad." The windows were tinted black.

I stopped. "It's not open."

Calvin kept walking. "Yeah, it is," he said, opening the door.

Inside, there were no customers. A pimply teen with dyed blond spiky hair was behind the counter, rapid-thumbing a Nintendo 3DS. We walked up to an old NEO-GEO cabinet, but the screen was black. The games had been unplugged. The kid said that if we bought tokens, he'd start up the machines. His English had a heavy Vietnamese quack. I used to be good enough to put a quarter in a game like Mortal Kombat and play for hours. I took out a dollar bill and asked the kid where the token machine was. He reached into a shelf below the register and pulled out a Tupperware full of tokens and said there was a twenty-dollar minimum.

"Who plays twenty dollars worth of arcade games?" I asked.

"Why you think there no one in here, doo?" the kid said.

I told him I used to work for Walt.

"Who dat?"

"Who owns this place now?"

"My uncle."

"Who's your uncle?"

"Who ack?"

"I used to play here all the time."

"He's DiggNiddy!" Calvin said.

"Twenty dollar, doo."

I eyed the dead games, statues commemorating a bygone time and place. The Arcade smelled of carpet mold. The mauve walls were badly in need of a fresh coat of paint, and there was an unpatched hole kicked into the side of the Street Fighter machine. In the back, a red curtain had replaced the door to the storage room. "What goes on back there?"

"We do gambling in here, nigga," the kid said. "Pok-uh, doo. We be selling banh mi so the playas can eat, doo."

"What about the games?"

The kid shrugged. "We play Xbox and PlayStation online."

I looked at Calvin, who shrugged.

"I feel old," I said. By the register, there was a stack of red business cards with golden Vietnamese words. All I could read was the phone number. I put one in my pocket.

As Calvin and I jogged back toward the funeral home through what was now pounding rain, I felt defeated. I wanted to show him the prize I'd won from my exile. Who needed Monterey Park and its insular, bull-headed, traditional Chinese culture when you could become the world's second-best gamer for a year? After I left home, I moved into a house with five guys in Pasadena and shared a room that was furnished with the latest and greatest in adolescent microbacteria. I went on training road trips to places such as Phoenix and Dallas and Kansas City and slept on the crumb-sprinkled floors of strangers I only knew by their handle. I'd often hear my father at night. No short cot in life. Work no fun; that's why it work. Now, years later, I still wanted to do something meaningful with my life. I just had no idea what that something was.

Back inside the funeral home, the attendees waited in line in front of Eddie's shrine to make another offering. The monks began to chant again. Their words sounded like music, an incantation. I could only understand a few phrases at a time. They said Eddie had five children and eight grandchildren and he was a good person and deserved a peaceful after-life. Was my father remembered the same way? Credited for the number of children and grandchildren he had, like a video game score. That meant my father's score was one. Did that mean he was suffering in the afterlife now?

The rain slapped the windows, sounding like tearing sheets of paper. The things we do to pretend we've healed. Move away from where you're from. Pocket a few extra dollars so you don't have to worry. Life's just a series of gaming levels consisting of split-second decisions you make based on how your mind interprets a few pixels of information. But in life when you mess up, there are no do-overs. How long did my mother hold that front door open to yell at me after I returned from Amsterdam? Two minutes? Five? When she said she never wanted to see me again, she couldn't have really meant never. I interpreted those moments incorrectly. If I had a chance to do it over—to replay that level—I wouldn't have turned tail. I'd have dropped my duffel and apologized. I'd have stayed on that doorstep until she let me in. I'd have done the right thing, even if my mother were too distraught to do the same.

Calvin's aunt found a way to get in line with Calvin and me. She called me by my Chinese name. "I can tell her to come," she said in Cantonese. "She made a mistake. She knows that. But you made one, too."

"Please, this is not your problem," I said in English.

"Dude, she's your mother," Calvin said. He said the word with the same level of reverence as he'd said my gaming handle.

"She cries for you every day," his aunt said.

In Cantonese I tried to say: then why hasn't she tried to find me? The words that came out were "why," "she," and "me."

Calvin's aunt clucked with exasperation. "So see-care!" she said in English.

We were handed incense sticks as we got to Eddie's shrine. I looked at his photo and told myself to get it together. Eddie was making me diagram my sentences. I lit the correct end of the incense stick this time. My palms met and I bowed. I inserted the offering into the urn with care, as gently as an acupuncturist would.

The monks rolled in Eddie's open casket. We lined up for the viewing. They banged a cowbell rhythmically like a heartbeat and led us as we snaked around the room several times before finally passing Eddie. He was wearing a silk skullcap and an embroidered red suit. He appeared small, asleep, and in peace. The color of his long and gaunt face was an unnatural waxy tan. People began to weep. Even big, Taylor Swift-loving Calvin. I can't say that Eddie and I were close. I can't say that my tears were all for him. But I couldn't stop my eyes from brimming, couldn't stop a few orphan tears from escaping.

The monks slowly unrolled a scroll that led to Eddie's shrine and asked a group of us to stretch the fabric taut. On the scroll, one of the monks laid a small plastic tray carrying a bowl of roast pork, a cup of tea, and a stack of paper money. The tray was passed slowly from one end of the fabric to the other. Calvin's aunt and I passed the tray to Calvin and his cousin's lover. They passed it on to the next set of hands. We did this until the tray reached Eddie's shrine, delivering a final takeout meal and a little pocket money for the afterlife.

About a month after the funeral, I called the owner of The Arcade and bought the place. I plan to make it a penny arcade with stations to play console games with friends. I'm going to name it "Eddie's Arcade," because had I not gone to the funeral that day, I wouldn't have met Calvin and his aunt. Had I not met Calvin and his aunt, I wouldn't be doing what I'm about to do.

Today, I drive to the old family house and park my car at the end of the street. I put on my sunglasses and through a pair of binoculars, I spy. After some time, my mother emerges, carrying a bag of mulch for a front garden I've never seen. She's grayer and smaller. Her gardening gloves cover the whole of her arms. I can still see the hardness in her, the way she walks with chopped, bowlegged steps, the pinched expression in her face, and her high, tense shoulders.

I'm going to get out of the car and walk up to the house. Then I'll take her to The Arcade to show her what I'm building. I'll show her the framed picture of Eddie Wu that will hang behind the counter. I'll tell her that Eddie was a friend who helped bring me home. I'll tell her that I haven't been angry, just scared, all this time and that I am ready to be her son again if she'll have me. I'm telling myself all this as my mother looks in the direction of my car, lifting her sun visor because she thinks she sees someone she recognizes.

I put down the binoculars so she can see my face. The car starts; we move forward.

10

The Bullet Points of Valley Pete

- Pete knows what the people in the office call him. Tool. Douchebag. Sycophant. He's heard it all before. As the head of global accounts, Pete is paid to ignore the prattle.

- Despite his lack of tangible accomplishments and the fact that he's worked for fifteen technology companies over the course of twenty-five years, Pete continues to be highly desired in The Valley. He has worked at several of the world's most admired Internet brands, and he has been an especially good drinking buddy to a sizable network of executives who will not hesitate to vouch for Pete's ability to "grow relationships." When he inevitably has to search for a new employer, he targets the companies that aspire to be the last one for which he worked. Say you're Google, for example. There are thousands of companies that want to be the *next* Google. If you show up on said company's doorstep saying you just worked for Google, eyes luminesce with desire.

- As he finishes his first year at this privately held

multi-billion-dollar (that's valuation; revenues are undisclosed) cloud computing company, Pete's enjoying the largest compensation package of his career, and yet he feels he's in trouble. He hasn't built enough alliances here. He's burned too many bridges in The Valley, which is a very small place. One of these days, someone he's torched will walk through the glass doors downstairs and be his boss or peer, and he or she will possess a long memory. He, like anyone else, would prefer to have a reputation as an inspirational leader and people manager, a high-performing professional, a winning father, a supportive husband—an all-around quality guy. But like the companies for which he's worked, in a final SWOT (Strengths, Weaknesses, Opportunities, Threats) analysis, change is more often driven by threats than opportunities.

- During his twenty-five-year career, Pete has done many things of which he's not proud:
    - The women. Mary, the buxom office manager with whom he had a three-year affair. The escorts in Hong Kong, Tokyo, and Singapore whose services were charged to his expense account. The boss he had on her knees in a London conference room. He has confessed nothing to his wife Jill. Why involve the children?
    - The enemies. Pete fabricates reasons to dismiss those he does not like. The senior

manager who found out about him and Mary. The inquisitive peer who discovered that the receipts for Pete's large client dinners hadn't originated from establishments that sold food. The list goes on. Pete devotes entire fiscal quarters to destroying others whose objectives are counter to his own.

- Steve, a vice president of U.S. accounts, walks glumly into Pete's corner office with the view of the flanks of other, taller buildings closer to Highway 101. Steve drops into the open chair and recites his weekly status report with all the passion of a robot dog low on batteries. He is prompted by a stapled sheaf of papers pocked with a seemingly endless list of bullet points. Pete does not like Steve. He is tall, dark-browed, handsome, and unlike Pete, he does not need to dye his hair. Pete can already tell that some of the younger, more attractive female employees would be open to an affair with Steve were he that type of man. Pete can tell Steve is that type of man. Because Pete is that type of man.
  - I'm worried I won't hit my number, Steve says. My top rep left for a competitor, and he'll take accounts with him.
  - Pete musters a shrug. When we ask you to hold a bag, we don't ask you to hold it until something bad happens. That's why we call them "quotas."

- Pete explains to his boss, the chief executive, that Steve and the reps he manages will not make their number this quarter and that Steve should ultimately be held accountable.
  - The chief executive asks: Aren't you ultimately accountable?

- Pete's son Johnson is lithe and athletic. He excels at soccer, football, and basketball. When Johnson was in Pop Warner and youth soccer, Pete enjoyed being a spectator. In recent years, however, Pete has missed most of Johnson's games. He blames business travel, but he's the one who strategically extends his trips so that he flies back on Saturdays instead of Friday nights. The truth is: Pete can no longer look his son in the eye because he reminds Pete of all the affairs he's kept secret from Johnson's mother. Now that his son is in high school, Pete doesn't enjoy waiting after games while he mingles with various friends. Many of them are attractive young women. Pete can easily imagine offering them internships at the company, summer jobs at minimum wage, just to have an excuse to swing by a lovely new intern's cubicle.

- Shiloh, Pete's daughter, looks like her mother used to. Long brown hair, wiry, bowlegged, so tall for thirteen that she slouches. In kindergarten, she'd habitually spread her legs and touch herself. At first, Pete found this act curious, watching his daughter as one might watch leopards bound across a desert on television.

Once, Shiloh began idly touching herself in front of houseguests, and Pete yelled at her to stop with an anger he didn't fully understand. These days, Pete asserts no such authority over Shiloh. She mostly ignores him before flouring her face with makeup. She's dating some pockmarked boy of South Indian descent with a ponytail and a harelip. Jill thinks he's nice. Pete knows better, as he did when the kindergarten-version of Shiloh spread her legs. Boys are never nice.

- Jill is unrecognizable to Pete. She's twice the size she was when they first met. Twenty years ago, she was his assistant. Now, he's secretly delighted that she prefers to skip office Christmas parties. When they have sex, he tries to remember what she looked like when she was thin. He never calls to mind any of the other women with whom he's slept during their marriage. Jill is the mother of his children; their lovemaking is sacred.

- On the way to his office, Pete eyes Steve leaning against a cubicle wall, laughing with a dark-haired woman in her late twenties whose crossed arms fail to hide that 1) she is well-endowed, and 2) she might be attracted to Steve. Pete finds a cubicle floor map and searches for the girl's name. Maeve Garner. Lovely.

- Alone in his office, Pete daydreams about piloting a

hang glider over The Valley, above the office parks and strip malls, above the playground where the kids at the nearby daycare center recess. When he was a child, Pete loved all things airborne. Planes. Space Shuttles. Superheroes. In his daydream, the children below point at him with admiration. Look at the man in the suit who can fly. They aspire to be him one day. The phone rings, and reverie vanishes. It's Pete's assistant, saying he's five minutes late to his biweekly staff meeting. He dials in, greets employees on three continents, and presents a single slide with bullet points that urge his team to stay focused on the following:

- Innovation
- Efficiency
- And most importantly, transformation

• While fielding questions from his staff, Pete mimics an oratory cadence that resembles Hollywood biopics about great speakers (*Malcolm X* he especially liked). He utters a variety of inaccuracies that he is unlikely to recall should he ever be asked to account for his answers in an executive team meeting or a court of law. After he hangs up, Pete feels drained. He removes his headset, goes to the window, and stares out at the office park across the street, searching futilely for his reflection in the glass of other buildings. That company is likely selling enterprise cloud services as well, and years from now, another large company will likely be selling yet another type of service targeted for other large companies. Every few months, Pete wants to quit, but the math quickly dissuades him. Jill doesn't work, and he promised to pay for college for both children. He has to hang on for at least another decade. He'll be fifty-eight then. When did his work begin to mean so little? He started his career as a junior sales manager making hardly any salary at all, existing only to inflate the commissions of the sales executive who hired him. His boss had hit his number twenty-four quarters in a row, and once he missed his number, he got fired, and Pete was promoted and given a modest compensation bump. Pete used to appreciate the heights to which he'd risen. Now, here on the seventh floor, Pete feels somehow that he's been at sea level for quite some time.

- Pete conjures a reason to visit the account management wing so he can swing by Maeve Garner's cubicle. Her hair looks tousled. Her face is flushed. Her gym bag is on her desk. She's wearing form-fitting running clothes the color of slate. Of course. Women such as her go on runs. Jill doesn't run. Men such as Pete never run; they stroll. They are followed.
    - Maeve says hi. From her peppy tone, Pete surmises that no one has called him a tool, douchebag, or sycophant in her presence. Unless she's a very good actor. Which she

157

has to be for her job. Maybe she's managing him like a needy account.

- ◦ Where do you run, Pete asks?
  - ▪ By the lake.
    - ▪ Me too. We should run together.

- • On the way home, Pete stops by a sporting goods store and purchases a pair of running shoes and shorts.

- • Maeve says she's a slow runner, but Pete is surprised he can keep up. His performance buoys his spirits. As they trot around the man-made lake, Pete tries to ignore the budding blisters caused by his new shoes. He also tries to avoid eye-feasting on Maeve's long, twig-like limbs, her narrow, blemish-free face, and her high cheekbones that billow like tiny sails. She has the perfect nose: in profile, an elegantly upended question mark. Pete asks a lot of questions, offers as little information about himself as possible, and definitely, absolutely, doesn't, under any circumstances, mention his family.
  - ◦ Maeve is twenty-eight.
  - ◦ Used to work as a lobbyist for a pharmaceutical company.
  - ◦ Currently single. Her boyfriend recently left her after five years.
  - ◦ Favorite musician is David Byrne. Pete tells her that, as an undergraduate, he saw Byrne

and the Talking Heads play for three hours at Madison Square Garden in the late 80s. He went to no such concert and has no idea whether such a show existed. In fact, he can't name a Talking Heads song.

- ○ After the run, Pete and Maeve glisten from exertion. When they pass by Steve in the lobby, Pete is the first to say hello.

- Pete takes his family to a beginner hang gliding lesson in nearby Milpitas, a town of 70,000 advantageously located at the intersection of the commuter highways 237, 680, and 880. Milpitas is the home of several thriving multi-billion-dollar conglomerate as well as the slowly dying computer hardware manufacturers that thrived in the 1980s.

  - ○ Inside the converted warehouse space, Johnson can't stop texting, and Shiloh has the gall to bring the Indian kid. Jill complains she's too big for the simulator. That's nonsense, the guide says. Pete remains silent.
  - ○ Pete straps into the harness, and the fan blows wind through his hair. He glides over digital foothills, but he imagines flying over The Valley, his office park, the daycare center. He waves to pointing spectators below. Maeve is among them.

- Pete and Maeve run three times a week. She is funny,

charming, intelligent, and perhaps most importantly, full of very specific life goals. She's saving money to travel to Southeast Asia. She plans to apply to the Peace Corps. One day, she wants to write a memoir about her experiences. To her, the company is merely a mediocre stopover town. The concepts of unfulfilled potential and regrettable acts you can't undo are strangers Maeve has no intention of ever meeting. Pete would be proud if Shiloh grew to be as brave and outspoken as Maeve. Later, when he is in the company gym's locker room changing back into his work clothes, the mere act of bending over to untie his running shoes makes Pete lightheaded enough to necessitate his sitting. He feels like the mediocre stopover town.

- Jill notices that Pete has lost ten pounds. He tells her that he runs the treadmill during lunch.
  - When you get to our age, you have to do more to keep the pounds off, Pete adds.
  - Jill stares hard at him.

- Pete knows that he and Maeve should stop running together. He has been through this enough times at enough companies to know where this is heading. Maeve has not asked once about Pete's family, though Pete has not removed his wedding ring. He estimates that he is a gift or two away from her bed. After watching Johnson win Most Valuable Player in the district soccer playoffs on Saturday, Pete is so proud of his son he can hardly breathe. He decides then and there that this running with Maeve must stop. Monday comes, and he schedules phantom meetings during the noon hour all week. He emails Maeve that their jogs are no-can-dos because it's near the end of the quarter. By Thursday, Pete has cleared his schedule, and he and Maeve are circling the lake again, beneath gliding, watching gulls.

- Pete goes on a hang gliding lesson alone. In the simulator, he flies off a large false hill. He imagines that he is flying over verdant and bosky New Hampshire, over the house where he grew up. It has green shutters, white shingles, and a large yard near a marsh and a reservoir. In the air, he misses his parents. Before dying nearly a decade ago, they had been schoolteachers, married forty years without infidelity. They used to frequently ask what Pete *really* wanted to do with his life, even after he became a vice president. When he and Jill had Johnson, Pete was supposed to start a company that helped make quality K-12 schooling more affordable. But the longer you do sales successfully, the more exponential the growth of the compensation, and the harder it becomes to abandon the life of a career salesman. Pete misses being seen as someone with potential. One day while his head is down and he's scrambling to make his number, his career will end. He won't know it at first. He'll think it's just a bump in the road and he'll catch on elsewhere. But when he interviews, Pete will be looked at like his first boss was looked at. Too old. Too high-priced. Too long since he worked at that Fortune 500. His references, retired. His Rolodex (the junior reps call it "network" now), worthless. As he brings his glider down, Pete plans to tell Maeve that one day she will miss being seen as someone with potential. By the time he lands, Pete decides he will tell Maeve no such thing.

- When Pete strolls into work, he sees Steve laughing at the entrance of Maeve's cubicle. Pete steps into the chief executive's office and explains that he will have to put Steve on a performance plan. The chief executive rises from his desk. Like Pete, he looks the part. Tall, broad-shouldered, served in the Army, and he didn't just serve in the Army, he played football; and he didn't just play football, he played quarterback. But he hasn't been CEO before, and it has been two years, and they've fallen short of growth targets so the pressure is on from the investors. When the chief executive asks Pete to shut the door, Pete knows he's in trouble.

- The following morning, Pete is on a performance plan. The chief executive has heard that Pete is more concerned with flirting with "the AM girls" than hitting his number.

- After telling Jill that he needs to spend a Saturday morning in the office, Pete meets Maeve for a hang gliding lesson. While Pete is in the harness, his simulator screen blacks out and the fans stop. Instead of feeling like he's flying, Pete just feels like he's dangling. He imagines his parents below, waiting to receive him. He assures Maeve that her flight will be more fun. At the end of the lesson, Pete invites her to a David Byrne concert in San Francisco, the tickets for which he had his secretary purchase.

- You're married.
  - But I adore you.

- You should know better.
  - Pete looks down at his shoes. For some reason, even though it's a Saturday, he expects to see his shiny leather wingtips instead of the fashion-deaf, insole-stuffed sneakers he's wearing. Even as he is, in fact, contrite, Pete also knows that he must appear as contrite as possible.

- I'm sorry, Maeve says. *We* should know better. I've been here before. It's something I want to change. Friends?
  - No point, Pete thinks.
  - Friends, Pete says.

- Maeve hugs Pete lightly, in a friendly way, like he's made of papier-mâché.

▪ Take your wife to the show, she says.

• On Monday, Pete sees Steve doing calf stretches on Maeve's cubicle wall. He's in running shorts. Even odds or better that they sleep together, Pete thinks. The walls of Pete's office are still bare. He hasn't even hung his framed diplomas from Stanford and Northwestern or the family portrait in which Pete appears to be the steeple of their modest chapel. He empties his desk drawers and puts the frames in a box. While staring down at the playground, he phones the executive recruitment agency. As Pete is being transferred to his headhunter, he daydreams of flying out over his home and above the children in his best suit, his shiniest dress shoes. The children point at him with admiration. They aspire to be him one day. The headhunter picks up.

   ◦ What can I do for you?

      ▪ I need to make a change.

11

Pyramid Schemes

1. Dim Sum

The day my father revealed what he had done, we were scheduled for one of our dim sum lunches. For us, dim sum equaled a progress report on how I was doing in school: first year of pre-law at Columbia.

He asked to meet at his office so we could carpool to the restaurant. The sky over South San Francisco was mottled with chrome-colored clouds that so transfixed me I shot through a red light and into an intersection, screeching to a belated halt. Luckily it was a Saturday, and there were no moving cars within miles of the many office parks in that area. Easing off the brake, I felt pushed forth as if by a strong wind.

The tower was empty of white-collar workers, but the janitors, doormen, and uniformed building security always worked weekends. The superintendent and I exchanged glances as he ascended a ladder to change a recessed halogen. He had worked in the building since I was a child. We recognized each other but had never exchanged a word. I didn't know his name.

I told the thick-necked fellow at the front desk that I was here to see my father—the man whose last name was on the side of the building—Eldridge Leong.

"Sure, dude, all the way up," he said.

I was wearing a T-shirt, khaki shorts, and flip-flops. I did not resemble someone who deserved to be called Sir.

I'd been all the way up to the fifty-fifth floor only a few times. Like a good executive, my father didn't spend many days behind a desk—he was usually out selling. When he was in his office, he seemed simultaneously lost and captive, unable to find pens and papers, spinning and expecting to topple some pricey accessory. The room was decorated by someone with taste (i.e., not my father). The walls were deep mahogany. The floors were glossy parquet, and the hanging light fixtures resembled golden gyroscopes. When I walked into my father's suite, the lights were flashing on and off.

"Not that one," he muttered. He was searching for the right switch.

My father's suit jacket was buttoned up so that he looked corseted around the ribs. Some salesman had convinced him this look—appropriate for a much younger man—was a good idea.

"What are you trying to do?" I asked.

He pointed skyward. "The whiteboard."

"Want me to try?"

"I've got it."

I reclined on the low-backed couch, which made all its backrest sitters look lazy and its edge sitters appear hyper-attentive. I kicked off my flip-flops and ran my toes through the pearl-white shaggy rug. It felt good. I was feeling good, hoping to get through the dim sum as quickly as possible, to unload my prepared, expedient lies.

My father finally found the right switch, and the white-board lowered. He then shut the blinds and dialed up the lighting. We were closed off to the outside. With a dry-erase marker, he drew a pyramid on the board. He wrote, "The Company" over the apex, "Real Estate Investment Trust (REIT)" beside one corner, and "The Investor" below the other.

To the right of the pyramid, my father wrote, "Us."

I don't recall how long he spoke. Felt like only a few minutes. I didn't fully understand everything he told me. I've never been particularly business-smart. But after all the lines were drawn, dotted, and labeled with dollar signs, even I could see that my father was describing conflicts of interest, fraud on a massive scale, undiscovered.

"Have I lost you?" he asked.

"No," I lied.

He erased the board. "Do you understand that you may be asked one day whether I disclosed this to you? And if you say yes, you could be held criminally liable?"

I told him that I understood, though I'm not sure I did at the time.

"Good," he said, "I hope you understand. Otherwise, I'm paying way too much for your law school."

Fine time to quip. "*Pre*-law," I corrected. I was pre-everything, just eighteen.

He explained that he had gone back and forth on whether to tell me. Ultimately he decided that I needed to be in on his big lie so I could make informed decisions to preserve my future. Informed decisions were a luxury not afforded to my father's hundreds of investors.

He capped his marker, holding it on both ends, staring at it. "You can also turn me in—if that's what you wish." Without the pen in his hands, it would have looked like he was holding his wrists out to be handcuffed.

I sat up on the couch. "Of course not, Dad."

After Mom died, I'd tried first and foremost to spare my father. He seemed to have aged ten years in five, graying and shrinking and sagging. Most notably, his voice had changed. He sounded like he was forever fighting a cold. My mother was only 42. It took me a very long time (and many sessions in a therapist's Upper West Side office) to feel the loss. She was the type of mother who always predicted that I'd fail. She felt strongly that I should have majored in business administration because she opined that since she immigrated to America, the government and the people had decided to anoint the institution of the corporation as its new organized religion. "Justice will be a quaint concept by the time you're old," she said. "You don't want to get stuck holding the door of a crumbling house." She was someone who enjoyed cutting down others just to watch them heal. But that day, on the fifty-fifth floor, my father was doing the cutting.

"Still want dim sum?" he asked.

I said I was no longer hungry.

---

2. Susan

I never got to tell my father those prepared, expedient lies. I was going to report that I was on track toward completing my requirements (and not just on track but excelling!), that I wasn't getting distracted by the new freedoms of university life (didn't even know what a bong was!), and that most importantly, I wasn't falling in love (since, as my father had said, love when you're young is a waste of time). The truth, like his Ponzi, was less tidy. I was on the verge of flunking out. After being a virtuous high-schooler, I had discovered the anesthetic joys of waking and baking. And of course, I was looking for love as if it was calling my name from an enchanted forest.

Where did I inherit my romantic tendencies? Certainly not from my parents. They were never particularly affectionate with each other or me. While my mother suffered her hospital treatments, the most affection my father showed was a pat on the back for both of us. He seemed to think his role was to play an ever-optimistic sports coach. When my mother finally passed away at home, my father's eyes were as dry as his jaw was stiff. Only years later did his front fall away. On that fateful dim sum Saturday, I avoided bringing up Mom because whenever I did, my father's eyes welled.

In college, I sought girls who were Mom's opposite. Sorry, Asian women. Materialistic ladies of suburban affluence? Out of the question. And women who wanted to mold me need not apply. I had a few lovers that first year. First Sara from my dorm—a Mexican girl who had a chip on her shoulder that rivaled the size of mine. I couldn't make sense of all her rants—initially about national politics, then about the many crimes she extrapolated from my preference for reticence. Then there was Emily and her lustrous Afro. She got me to volunteer as a Big Brother out in the Bronx. I'd discover that while I was out at the playground with my Little Brother, the kid's mom was always home smoking weed. It didn't take me very long to start flaking on the boy, and soon thereafter, on Emily.

Finally, there was Susan. Without her glasses on, she was

the most beautiful woman I'd ever seen, with thickly lashed green eyes, perfect teeth (an orthodontic success!), and pale skin bearing an almost invisible layer of down. She was a friend of my roommate and best male friend Aiden, a tall, affable business major with whom I shared sporting-team and alcoholic-beverage allegiances. Susan's father was a Nobel Prize-winning chemist. Her older brother was a mathematician at MIT. The family expected a similar level of achievement from their daughter, who was a chemistry major. Susan was the only person I knew who carried expectations as weighty as mine.

One night, with fake IDs, we sneaked into a crowded bar on West End Avenue. Aiden, because of his height, looked much older than he was. While he tried to wedge his way to the taps, Susan and I waited at the stand-up tables by the window. She plucked the ketchup out of the steel condiment carrier and began rolling the bottle back and forth in her palms. Her mind was often elsewhere; she was not a person who made good eye contact.

I commented on how Aiden was a full head and shoulders taller than the throng at the bar. Susan's smile flickered like the lights in my father's office. The rolling of the bottle intensified. I began thinking about Susan's breasts, which aside from her emerald eyes were the most profound of her physical gifts.

"Do you think there's a predictive part of our brains?" Susan said. "Like we basically know in the back of our heads how things are going to end? Not in a psychic way, but in an intuitive sense?"

"I don't see how."

"Where do you think you'll be in fifteen years?"

I told her that I imagined myself as a lawyer, miserable and alone. But I wasn't really telling her everything. I imagined myself being heartbroken by someone like Susan.

She put down the ketchup bottle and rested a hand on my shoulder. "That's so sad. You're not alone now. So what data point gives you the idea that you will be?"

I revised my descriptions of her. She had many physical gifts. Her face was long, her chin narrow. Her hair was shoulder-length, lustrous. I felt ugly in comparison.

"My mother passed away a couple of years ago. Cancer. A miserable death." Immediately, I wished I hadn't revealed that. What a fucking downer! Aiden was on his way with our drinks, a stout tree bearing alcoholic fruit, two hands bracketing three glasses. I didn't even want to drink anymore for fear of more honesty spewing forth at Susan, this woman I saw in my future, this woman I'd try to make happy until she found someone she saw in her future—probably someone who looked like Aiden.

"We won't be alone," she said, removing her hand from my shoulder as Aiden approached. "We'll be left with the burdens of our families."

How did she know these things? How did either of us know anything at all? We were just children!

Love when you're young is a waste of time, I'd tell my son fifteen years later.

———————

3. Going Dutch on Our Daddy Cards

A few weeks after my father revealed his secret, Susan and I were up on the roof deck of the apartment building where she shared a two-bedroom with four girls. It was a clear day; we could see down from Washington Heights to the Freedom Tower. The buildings were like rock formations. In Manhattan, people fooled themselves into thinking that they could own their small piece of this island, when in fact, over time, their mortgage payments went to people like my father who gave it to good-for-nothing children like me to spend on beautiful rich children like Susan. The people who owned Manhattan were really investing in us. They should have been disappointed.

Susan hiked her glasses and sighed. "Why can't we do this all the time?"

"That'd be odd," I said. "Millions of people on rooftops staring."

Susan smiled but then went quiet. "Push comes to shove, that's what we do. Stare. My dad stares at me like he used to look at my mom. Back when he trusted her." She then revealed that her mother had been with another man, a married one, for at least a decade.

"She's a fraud," she said.

"I know fraud."

She took off her glasses and we kissed. Her lips were soft but cold. I kept my eyes open because I didn't want to forget her face. When we were done, I immediately wished I had kissed her harder, with greater conviction—more heart.

I touched a lock of hair that rested on her shoulder. She wrapped an arm around my waist and laid her head against my chest. She smelled of hair and sun. We looked out at the city as if our future was out there, and we were unafraid.

"I want to take you to an expensive dinner and eat like it's our last night on Earth," I said.

"If it's the last night on Earth, wouldn't it be because we ate all the food already?"

I made reservations at a Michelin-starred restaurant on Central Park South. I insisted on ordering the tasting menu with the wine pairing. I wore my only suit and tie, the one I'd worn to senior prom. Under a winter coat, she wore a green strapless dress that looked like it belonged to her mother. It was a little too big, and the hem was a little low on her legs.

"I've got my card," I said. By "my card," I meant my father's, which I surfaced for especially costly purposes like textbooks, tuition, and my soon-to-be perjuring soul.

"I've got my card, too," Susan said. By her card, she also meant her father's.

"We can go Dutch on our dads."

"Aiden would call us out," she said. "One-percenters."

Aiden's father was running for City Council. He was spending two nights a week flyering outside supermarkets and subway stations in the outer boroughs. Though Aiden had grown up in Manhattan, his parents were from Queens, and his grandfather was a cop. I wished I wasn't thinking about Aiden, wished Susan hadn't brought him up.

"His family owns a lot of property here," I pointed out. "Aiden's dad is O.G. Manhattan. Old Gold. Pretty funny that he's now running like he's Mr. Blue-Collar-From-The-Outer-Boroughs."

"At least he's trying," she said. "You have to do what you can. If you can't even do that, then you shouldn't have the right to judge."

I felt myself coloring. Susan plucked at her napkin and wiped nothing. The amuse-bouche came. I couldn't help but apply Susan's words to my situation with my father. Should I blow the whistle? If I didn't have the courage, was I complicit in his crimes?

"I don't know what this is," I said, gesturing at the space between her and me. "I mean, I know what this is to me. I don't know what this is to you."

Susan looked at me like I was dumb. "Why don't you just ask?"

Outside the restaurant later, in front of one of those fancy hotels, we embraced with an urgency many wouldn't attribute to a scientist's daughter and a real estate man's son. Hands over bodies, teeth clicking, tongues searching for truth. We would wake together.

When I bring back these memories, I try to slow the time down, to recall more than fragments.

Sometimes I wonder if I'm making moments up—cooking the books like my father.

---

4. The Fix

My father called to tell me he planned to end his pyramid scheme. He had found a way to finance the fix. It involved his associate's connection to the head of one of the leading polysilicon producers in China and the Chinese government's generous solar energy subsidies. He was off to the Henan Province in the morning.

"We're going to get out of this, I promise," he said. "You can't have it both ways in life. I know. I've tried. Remember my lesson."

I wanted to say that my father had ceded his right to teach

me lessons when he involved me in his fraud. I had been doing my homework. There was no mathematical way out of a Ponzi. You could continue to fund the promised returns to your Ponzi investors using a separate legitimate operation, but the whole reason you start the scheme is because you're too lazy to endure the ups and downs of a legitimate business. The only way out was to get caught or vanish.

"I don't know what you want me to say, Dad," I replied.

He was quiet for a long time. I wasn't about to give him the satisfaction of snapping the silence.

"It started small," he said, "just to cover up a bad year. I was over-leveraged on a commercial development. Your mom had her treatments." My father released a sigh, but I could tell he was choking up. I started to think I wouldn't make it another fifteen years. I wouldn't even get to miserable and alone.

"Are you still there?" he said.

"I am."

"Then wish me luck."

I did as my dad asked, though we didn't deserve it.

---

5. Aiden

Strong male friendships have been rare for me. I didn't realize how rare until after college. After Aiden.

Few of my memories at Columbia excluded him. We hit it off immediately in the dorms. We came from different places. He was white; I am Chinese. I was a class clown—the kid in the back of the room making snide remarks under his breath. Aiden was a jock, an A.P. scholar in cheerleader-fucking. He brought home some of the tallest, hottest women I had ever seen. I told myself that there was no way Susan was his type. Her weight fluctuated; she carried those small fleshy balloons above the belt. They would have looked like a strange match; Susan was half as tall as Aiden. He was also never friends with the women he slept with.

There are two types of male friendship. The first type is the like-like. Both men connect because they have a lot in common. Subconsciously, they either fear difference or they lack curiosity about others. The second type of friendship is the be-like. One of the men wants to be like the other. I wanted to be like Aiden.

Aiden and I played the latest *Call of Duty* like divorced parents. In separate bedrooms in the same apartment, we were attached to our consoles. We spoke over headsets. He asked how things were going between me and Susan.

"OK," I said. "I think she's happy."

"You think?"

"How can we ever know?"

"Sometimes she tells you, and other times you ask."

Aiden liked to game-theory every problem into two or three chewable decision points.

We were chasing some terrorist leader through a series of alleys in a cartoon Beirut. Aiden started blowing me up just for laughs. I started blowing him up just for laughs.

"You're my desert bitch!" I shouted.

"'Fuck you' in Arabic!"

That made me laugh so hard I couldn't play anymore.

"Come on, dude," Aiden said, "the terrorists are getting away."

"Just order an air strike."

"Lame."

He ordered an air strike, which magically reduced the number of bad guys to which we had to lay waste.

"Your dad would be very upset at the potential civilian losses of that decision," I said.

"Fuck you in English."

"Sorry, I couldn't resist."

"My dad is the real deal."

"He's never done anything shady?" I said. "He's a politician. Come on."

"Look, I don't know. He's not Jesus. But he's an adolescent politician, basically. If he has done anything, he'd cop to it. Because eventually the truth finds a way out."

The storm clouds of my father's decisions came over me.

Aiden paused our game. "I'm happy for you and Susan."

I thanked him. "What do you think of her?"

"She's gotta be the smartest person I know."

"What about me, motherfucker?"

"Well, you haven't told her you love her yet."

Susan told Aiden that?

I un-paused our game and rushed forward into our next map, taking the lead in clearing out terrorists. But I went too fast, leaving Aiden behind. Before he could offer me cover, the bad guys ambushed, and I died.

"I'm afraid of losing her," I admitted as our map reloaded.

I expected Aiden to ask why I was afraid.

"To whom?" he said instead.

---

6. The Bottom of The Well

Susan, Aiden, and I pretended like we had no money on Fridays. We'd put our Daddy Cards away, buy groceries and a cheap bottle of Trader Joe's wine, and we'd cook in.

One night in Susan's room, the three of us added a brick of hashish to our plebeian recipe and streamed *The Big Lebowski*. Stoned to the point I hallucinated the floor disappearing, I was sandwiched between Aiden and Susan on the flattened living-room futon. I eyed the foothill of her hip and wanted it against my palm, tucked against me. But with Aiden's long body at my back like an endless log, I didn't dare. If I made a move, would this friendship end?

John Goodman had just tried to cast his dead friend's ashes to the sea, only to have them blown back into his face. Susan and Aiden's laughs had the same rhythm. They practically harmonized with each other. Yes, I was very stoned.

I closed my eyes and thought that if my father failed to finance his way out of his Ponzi, then I'd propose that I change my name to The Dude. The room keeled, and I fell asleep. I dreamed of sitting alone at the bottom of a well, the walls cold, dry, and harsh like pumice. Only Aiden's raspy machine-gun laughter and Susan's smell reminded me of the world above. I touched the silky surface of the puddle, which turned into the bowling lane from the dream sequence in *The Big Lebowski*. I was on my back, floating down the approach, heading toward a pin deck with no pins. The widening pit. A woman's spread legs appeared. I passed between them and stared up her skirt, only to see the triangle of sky at the top of the well. I heard snores buzzing, rhythmic moans making the hair on my arms stand. Was I having a wet dream? With my best friends in the same bed?

I woke, still in Susan's place, frightened I'd be talking dirty or touching myself. It was dark and cold. The floodlight outside her ground-floor apartment had blown out. A red glow flickered from the alarm clock. It read 3:54 AM. Susan and Aiden were gone.

---

7. The Spelling of Truth

Aiden was out campaigning again for his father. For a better, more accountable city. For better, more accountable people at "the top of society's pyramid." Susan and I were playing Scrabble at our place. By ours, I meant Aiden's and mine. I was in a foul mood. Susan seemed unusually reticent and her eyes were red. She was probably stoned. I whiffed the stale air around her as I walked past for a beer. She definitely smoked out earlier. Without me. Did Aiden fire up her bong? I led our game by at least 100 points, destroying her. The winner's prize? The truth, I told myself.

When I sat again, I played the word "ABLE."

"Now you play Cain," I joked.

"Cain's not a word," she said, sounding annoyed.

"We don't have to play," I said.

Susan began to sniffle. I had been wrong. She had been stoned and crying. She wiped tears off her chin with her wrist.

"What's the matter?"

"I can't," she kept saying.

"Can't what?"

She began to cry harder. I got up and put my arms around her. She clasped my forearms like they were protectors on a roller coaster. A tear fell and spread against my sleeve. My chest felt hard. *Tell me you cheated on me. Tell me you're a fraud, too.*

"My mother wants a divorce," she said. "She wants to marry that other guy. She said she doesn't love my father anymore."

"Oh," I said, unable to sap the many feelings other than empathy from my tone. Relief. Distrust.

Later on, we were in my bed, and instead of initiating a conversation about us, instead of asking her about the future, I unburdened myself about what my father had done and how I was expected to help him cover it up by staying quiet.

Susan was motionless in my arms for a long time. I asked her to face me. The life in her eyes drained like she was running low on batteries. I wanted to know what she was thinking, I said, but I wasn't sure if I really did want to know. She managed to force a laugh that sounded like a tower of building blocks crumbling.

"You shouldn't have told me that," she said.

———

8. The Price of Rice in the Henan

My father flew directly from China to New York to visit me. He asked to meet for dim sum in Chinatown. I warned him the Chinese food in Manhattan sucked, but I knew he wasn't visiting to eat. When I asked him how things had gone in China, he chirped "Good!" and left it at that. A portentous response.

We met outside the #6 train Canal Street stop. A wave of pedestrians and street hawkers flowed between us when I came above ground and spotted him. He looked around and swallowed distastefully.

"You took the subway?" he asked.

"People do that here."

He inhaled and buttoned his blazer. I led him in the direction of Chinatown. I felt power in having my father follow me for once. Then he looped the straps of a surgical mask over his ears.

"What?" he said, when he saw me staring at him.

"How was the Henan?" I asked again.

"Amazing," he said. "It's a new frontier out there. Anything is possible. Not like here."

He had to have known I didn't actually care about the price of rice in the Henan.

"I have some important meetings lined up here this week."

That's how I knew that my father's trip had not gone well and that the Ponzi was still going.

"You should cop to it," I said. "Admit what you did."

My father laughed. With his mask on, it looked like he was hunched and coughing.

"You said you couldn't have it both ways."

"You can't be both illegitimate and legitimate," he said.

"You can't do wrong and not take accountability."

"Yes, you can't do that and be free."

When people said you couldn't have it both ways, what did they mean?

"Aren't they teaching you anything in law school?" my dad said.

We passed the police precinct on Elizabeth Street. I grabbed my father by the elbow and led him toward the station.

"What are you doing?" he asked.

"We're turning ourselves in."

My father shook free and stopped. "Are you crazy? We don't have a plan yet."

"You can't get out of this!" I said. "There's no way out."

"It started small," my father mumbled. "We had one bad year. And your mom had her treatments."

"Stop!" I said. "I know what happened. I was there. Don't blame Mom."

My father sighed. His mask ballooned. He flipped his gray bangs. "We're not ready," he said, backpedaling. "We're not ready." He turned and walked briskly away from me and around the corner. I chased after him. By the time I peeked down Canal Street, my father had broken into a full sprint. I started running, only to see him vanish into a cab heading uptown.

---

9. Account-A-Billy

Susan and I volunteered for one of Aiden's flyering events. Susan's idea, of course. We stood outside a Key Food supermarket in Brooklyn Heights and offered handbills asking residents to Vote For Account-A-Billy. Bill Chambord had been the VP of Finance for three decades at a global bank.

Even though Aiden was stopping every outgoing shopper, he managed to say, "Vote for my Dad" like he meant it each time.

Susan got attention with her smile and her enthusiasm for our friend. She never drifted further than a few steps away from Aiden all morning. I'd never seen her smile as widely for me.

I tried to rise above my messy feelings and campaign for

Aiden's dad. I couldn't stop thinking about how I must have looked like a coward in Susan's eyes compared to Aiden. There he was, shilling fearlessly for his father. Then there was me. Chilly. Bottled up. Shedding tears for no one. Not my dead mother. Not my father. Not my father's investors. Not even for the girl with whom I was purportedly in love.

I went for a pee, disappearing into the stock room through two heavy rubber curtains. In the restroom, mopping buckets filled with dark water surrounded the toilet, which didn't have a seat. I deserved such a place.

When I returned outdoors, I saw it. Susan's arm around Aiden's waist and Aiden gazing down into her eyes like a staged wedding photo. They detached before they saw me. One could construe the contact as casual, even innocent. But it was there—the spark of parallel lives intersecting. Even if Aiden did possess the utmost respect for my relationship with Susan, he at least imagined, at least entertained, the notion. And she did, too.

That night, a FedEx package waited for me at the dorm. From my father. Alone in the room, I opened it. Instructions to visit a man in Jersey City who would help me forge a new identity. I put the papers on my desk beside a VeloBound reader for my Criminal Justice 1 class.

---

10. Romantic Tendencies

I waited outside Susan's apartment for thirty-five minutes while she made her way back from campus. I asked her on a grown-up date; this time I'd bought us tickets to the opera at Lincoln Center. The streetlights were flashing reds. There

I was, sitting on the stoop of her brownstone, wearing my only suit again, holding a mixed bouquet of dahlias (chosen because they were priciest that time of year). When Susan appeared around the corner, her glasses had slipped down the bridge of her nose. She was rushing with a lean book bag slung over one shoulder; she looked to me like someone running from—not toward—adulthood. We were going to miss the opera.

When she saw me, she pouted her lips. "I am so sorry," she said, kissing me on the cheek.

I told her it was OK. These days I would feel a twinge about the $200 I'd spent on those tickets. But back then, I was just my Daddy Card. I was, in fact, the card he played to make himself feel like a good person. I handed her the flowers and relieved her of the weight she carried.

She stared at the dahlias and rolled the bouquet back and forth in her hands. The bulbs jiggled like baby's flesh. I would think about them when my son was born. Susan closed her eyes and sniffed them, even though, as I've since discovered, dahlias don't smell.

"What do you want to do?" she said. "Get dinner? Grab a drink? Stay in?"

"Whatever you want to do."

"Want to call Aiden?"

I felt like I would stand there on this Washington Heights sidewalk, in front of this apartment, forever, carrying other people's things, holding the door of crumbling houses, watching people pass me by.

"I love you," I said.

She adjusted her glasses. Her eyes, magnified, moistened.

There was something in the way her lips flattened and jaw stiffened that made me regret what I'd said.

We kissed and she thanked me "for everything," like she'd never receive anything else from me again.

---

11. With Conviction

My father turned himself in shortly after Susan left me and started dating Aiden. By the time the snow began to fall on Manhattan, he had been sentenced to twenty-five years in federal prison for defrauding over 200 investors of $52 million. Before he turned himself in, he sent me a postcard of San Francisco without a message. That was the agreed-upon signal in his instructions to go to his man in Jersey City. I dropped out of Columbia, changed my name, and moved back to San Francisco. Ned Leong became Ed Chang, who would enroll at a community college. Ed is just Ned with a shaved head. Ed transferred to UC Berkeley and majored in Political Science. Ed is now a paralegal at a law firm in downtown San Francisco.

In his plea allocution, my father apologized to the victims of his crimes, but he apologized to me first for leaving me "a legacy of shame." He made clear that although the company was a family business that he intended me to inherit, I never knew about his Ponzi. My father had spared me.

I was in a relationship with a woman I met in community college. We were together for seven years, cohabitated, had a son, who is now nine. She left me last year because every day was the same. I never surprised her, rarely took her on dates, was emotionally secretive. She once said I didn't have a romantic bone in my body.

----

12. The Chambords

I learned about Aiden and Susan's marriage online. Their wedding pictures looked beautiful. I'd come up with more descriptive words, but the effort would hurt too much. They seem happy. But everyone seems happy on social media. Some experts say Aiden's next political step is to run for mayor. Susan is a professor at Columbia. They have two children.

I'm tempted to add them as friends. Who's this Ed Chang guy, they'd ask? Then they'd recognize my profile picture. Then they'd send a message.

"Is that you, Ned?" *What the fuck happened to us?*

I'd reply that, in the back of my brain, way back when my father first told me about his pyramid scheme, way back when the three of us began our triangle in that Washington Heights apartment, deep down, my intuition predicted how we would end.

About the Author

A MacDowell Colony fellow, Leland Cheuk is the author of the novel *The Misadventures Of Sulliver Pong* (CCLaP Publishing, 2015), which was an Amazon National Bestseller in Asian-American Literature. Cheuk's work has appeared in publications such as *Salon, Electric Literature, The Rumpus, Kenyon Review, Prairie Schooner,* and elsewhere. He lives in Brooklyn.

Thought Catalog, it's a website.

www.thoughtcatalog.com

Social

facebook.com/thoughtcatalog
twitter.com/thoughtcatalog
tumblr.com/thoughtcatalog
instagram.com/thoughtcatalog

Corporate

www.thought.is